The Amygdala Defense

A Novel by

E.W. Chandler, B.S., J.D., LL.M

ISBN 978-1-7367908-0-9

Front cover image: Four U.S. Marines, from the author's archives.
Photo on Author's page from the author's archives.
Back cover photo from the author's archives appeared in *The Jackson Sun*, Madison County, Tennessee, 1980.

First printing 2021.

Layout and design by
Wind Song Press
windsong@mtnhome.com

Published in the United States
by Beyond Elementary, 2021.

Please direct inquiries to:
Edward Witt Chandler
wittdaux@gmail.com

Dedication

*Each of us is more
than the worst thing we've ever done.*

—Bryan Stevenson

Bryan Stevenson is an African-American lawyer born in 1959 in Delaware. In 1985, he graduated from Harvard Law School. He is a professor at New York University School of Law and the founder and executive director of Equal Justice Initiative in Montgomery, Alabama. His work as a lawyer over the years challenging bias against the poor and minorities in the criminal justice system, as well as his defense of those facing the death penalty, is remarkable, but it was his particular concern as an advocate for the rights of children accused of crime that inspired me.

Edward Witt Chandler, March 2021

Table of Contents

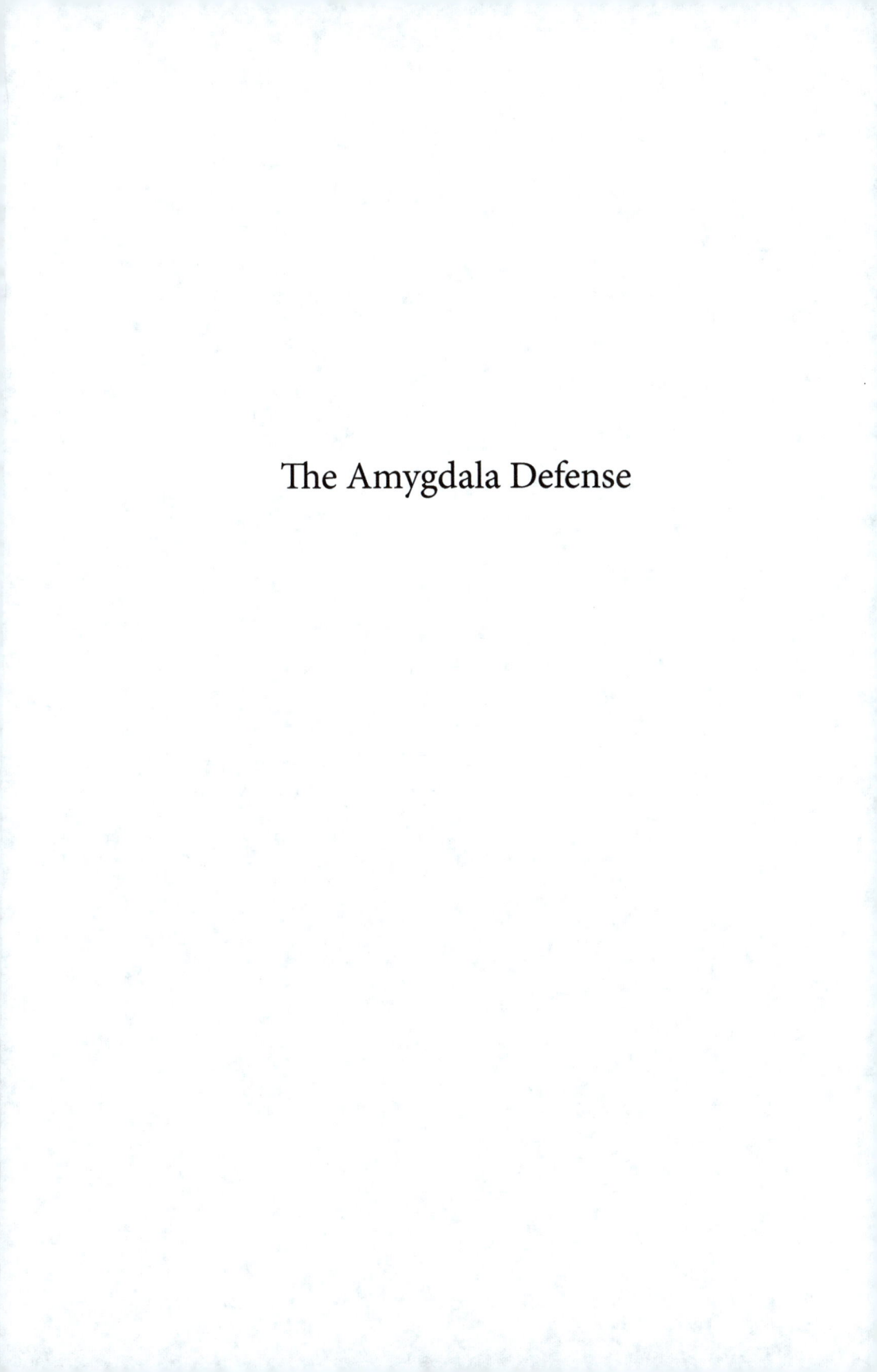

The Amygdala Defense

Chapter 1

Christmas Eve 2004, Friday
The Jack Pen
Memphis, Tennessee
Murder

The knife struck him in the heart, and he fell with a thud. The woman behind the bar saw what happened and fled out the back door, escaping into an alley. The man with the knife dropped it beside the body and left through the bar's entrance.

Down the alley the woman ran, until she came to a pink neon sign that said OPEN. Inside, she dialed 911 and told the operator to send the police. There had been a killing. "The Jack Pen," she said. "805 South Main." It was 2 o'clock a.m. Snow was falling. Large flakes floated to the ground. It was very cold. She returned to the bar and stood by the entrance, afraid to enter.

The jukebox in the corner that had been playing an Elvis Presley song had stopped. Bruce Voltz, Marine veteran, had drunk his last beer. His body lay lifeless on the floor. The siren of a Memphis police car began to wail, coming closer and closer.

The police finally arrived.

"He's dead," said Dusty Jones, himself a veteran. He recognized Bruce.

The woman followed them in and moved behind the bar, fear in her eyes. "He didn't do nothing, officer," she said. "Bruce and Willie were arguing. Willie was eating a steak I had cooked for him. They were right there. Bruce began to light a cigarette, and suddenly he called Willie a 'nigger.' Willie just struck him. Right there. See the knife? There's the cigarette and the match. He never got it lighted."

By that time, crime scene officers had arrived, and tape was being strung across the door. A small crowd gathered on the sidewalk. Then the ambulance arrived, and after photos were taken, the body was removed and taken to the Shelby County Medical Examiner's Office, a few miles down Madison Avenue.

The woman gave them her name.

"Sally," she said. "Sally Faye. My dad was Duke Smith. He opened this bar in 1952. But he died a year ago. I've been trying to operate it myself, seven days a week, 24 hours a day. Old men who talk about sex, think about it, and do little more besides get drunk. Most are veterans."

She sobbed. "Bruce was my dad's best friend. He was a lot younger, but they had been fishing buddies. Now they're both gone." She cried quietly, and then she finally spoke. "Willie came to the bar frequently, but I never knew his last name until Friday. It was Armstrong. Willie Armstrong."

Chapter 2

December 27, 2004, Monday
Office of John Alexander
Memphis, Tennessee
Willie Armstrong

The seventeenth floor of the Lincoln American Tower was the Memphis office of John Alexander. He'd been practicing criminal defense for almost 40 years. His uncle had been a lawyer and his grandfather before that. They were the oldest criminal defense firm in Memphis, Tennessee. They were also one of the smallest firms except for the solo practitioners.

After John's grandfather died and before John finished law school at Vanderbilt in Nashville, his uncle had struggled by himself trying to keep the business afloat until his nephew arrived. It had been a financial struggle for both of them, but mostly because John insisted on teaching criminal law as an instructor at the University of Memphis and wasn't the businessman his uncle was. When his uncle died of prostate cancer, John struggled on, but he knew he would have to give up teaching. Money had to come first.

The phone rang. It was 8:00 a.m., and his secretary, Ann Kimberly, hadn't arrived yet. John answered the phone.

"Hello. Alexander Law Firm. How may I help you?"

"My name is Willie. Willie Armstrong. I'm in bad trouble." The man sounded distraught.

"What's this about, Mr. Armstrong?" asked John, trying to talk and drink his Starbucks coffee at the same time.

"I'm wanted for murder in Memphis. I'm hiding in Florida." He was quiet.

John perked up. He loved murders. They meant money. *There is always a defense to murder*, he remembered his grandfather saying.

3

"Well, Mr. Armstrong, give me your phone number. I'll contact the police and call you back."

"No. You call the police, and I'll call *you* back in one hour. But I'm telling you, they want me for the murder at the Jack Pen in Memphis. It's been in all the papers. My grandmother called me."

"Fine. Call back in one hour. Incidentally, if this is murder, it will cost money—lots of money."

"My grandmother has it. I'll send her to you." He paused a moment. "How much?"

John's mind raced. "Maybe $100,000 cash up front."

"I'll get it. I must be found not guilty. Do you understand?" He waited for John's response.

John said nothing for just a beat. Then he said, "Yes," and hung up.

Chapter 3

December 27, 2004, Monday
Office of John Alexander
Memphis, Tennessee
The Amygdala Defense

Captain Josh Williams had retired after a lifetime of policework, but he continued to work for the Alexanders because he just couldn't quit. They called him an "investigator," but really he was the "information man."

He had the police connections.

After he read the police report, he copied it on the Memphis police headquarters Xerox machine.

"Thanks, Gomer," he said to the desk sergeant. "See you later." He returned the report, stuffed the copy into his pocket, and left the building.

Soon, in John's office, the two men sat quietly while John read the report with another cup of black coffee in his right hand.

"Get some coffee, Josh," John mumbled as he read.

And then it hit him. He jumped out of his chair. "Oh... my...God. Oh, my God! It's the amygdala defense!"

Josh almost laughed.

"It's perfect. It's perfect!" For ten years John had been teaching the amygdala defense, but so far, in hundreds of reported cases, no murder had the facts. There were no reported cases in the entire United States or anywhere. He was beside himself.

Josh didn't know what John was so excited about, and so he said nothing. The phone rang. This time Ann answered and buzzed. "There is a Mr. Armstrong on the line for you."

John beamed. His dream had come true.

Chapter 4

January 6, 2005, Thursday
A motel room
Orlando, Florida
A good and honest man

Willie stared at the wall of his motel room in Orlando, beginning to seriously consider what was going to happen. Ever since he had graduated from U.S. Marine recruit training at Parris Island, South Carolina, he had worked hard to be a good and honest man.

Granted, he had been a juvenile delinquent, but within three months of graduating from high school in Memphis, he had decided to join the U.S. Marines. Granted, after he retired from the Marines, he continued to drink like a fish and had become an alcoholic.

He began to cry. Murder. Charged with *murder*. How would this lawyer defend him? He wasn't insane, and intoxication wouldn't be his defense. Sure, he was an alcoholic, like his father, but he knew what he did, knew the difference between right and wrong.

So why had he exploded? He'd been called "nigger" many times—in boot camp at Parris Island, infantry school, airborne training, and in the Army Ranger training program in Georgia. Even after he got his commission as a second lieutenant and was a platoon leader in the 4th Marines, he had ignored the racial slurs. He hated the word "nigger." On the street he would not tolerate it. But murder?

He could have punched the man in the mouth. Bruce was a Marine buddy, too. It didn't make sense. And why had Bruce called him a nigger? He'd been so drunk, he didn't really remember the conversation.

Chapter 5

January 15, 2005, Saturday
Office of John Alexander
Memphis, Tennessee
Ida Armstrong

John Alexander had spent the night tossing and turning in his bed until he finally got up at 4:00 a.m. to watch the news on TV.

The amygdala defense. It was a dream come true. He had written a paper on it that had been published by the Tennessee Criminal Defense Lawyers, but it had drawn very little interest from other lawyers—some of whom complained that the system was at least fifty years away from such a defense.

How stupid. If it was a defense, just get an expert, a neurobiologist, who knew the difference between the conscious and the unconscious mind and was willing to be an advocate of a new defense. Who would that be? Maybe he'd call the University of Tennessee School of Medicine or St. Jude's Hospital today and see.

Or should he wait until "Mr. Green" arrived? A lump sum of cash of $100,000. He had already spent the money in his mind. Redo the kitchen, the baths, take a family vacation to Cancún. Maybe buy a 30-ton fishing vessel in Alaska and do that fishing he dreamed of.

He hardly paid any attention to the TV. The news was boring, and this new challenge was on his mind—the amygdala defense.

After a shower, breakfast, and coffee, and while driving through heavy traffic on the way downtown, he began to organize his thoughts. The amygdalae were located in the temporal lobes. He was mentally drawing a picture for the jury: the frontal, parietal, temporal, and occipital lobes.

As he sat at a traffic light, he took the palm of his right hand and put it up against the side of his head, closing his fist, thumb inside. Then he brought his hand back down and opened the four "covering" fingers, leaving his thumb in his palm. The amygdala was like an "almond" at the tip of his thumb, only there were two, one on each side of the brain. Two amygdalae. Just an area of the brain.

When Willie struck with the knife, it was likely instantaneous. And he had an eyewitness who had said so, according to the newspaper. He had to talk to Willie before the police did, to make sure he was not pressured to change his version of the killing.

On the other hand, the police would not mess with those facts. They didn't know the difference. Better Willie talk to the cops first without any advice. He would have the police pick Willie up at his office before an interview, work out a bail bond for his release from jail, and then let the cops get a taped statement. After that, Willie could come back to his office for the interview. Good plan, but it was dangerous.

Should he "lecture" Willie first?

As Alexander pulled into the parking lot, he decided to have Willie's grandmother bring the fee money that day. He could have the captain take a statement as to Willie's birth, childhood, and Marine military history, as best she could relate.

As he walked toward the elevator of the Lincoln American Tower on the way to his office, John returned to the theory of the defense, which was a criminal defense lawyer's most important task. A criminal lawsuit was like an iceberg. Seven-eighths was hidden from view. What went on in the courtroom was only one-eighth of the work.

Investigation, preparation, and theory development was paramount to a successful defense. The word "nigger" had lit up the amygdala. The amygdala had made the decision to kill. The cerebral cortex, where human decisions ordinarily take place, was not involved. The decision to kill was not a conscious decision.

But how would he convince twelve jurors? Those who were religious (believed in God, heaven, hell, the Devil) would be the hardest. They also believed in free will. He needed a jury consultant and a juror questionnaire. Weed these people out as much as possible. Call that jury consultant he'd used successfully last year. Helen Anderson. He thought she had moved to California. He would get her back. It was a matter of money. She was the best.

In his office, he opened his mail and called Willie's grandmother. The fee money was on its way, and Willie would arrive the next day. He would have the captain pick Willie up at the airport, and then they would all meet with the police in his outer office or the conference room.

On the wall in John's office was a framed drawing of a dog, with big black letters:

A CRIMINAL DEFENSE LAWYER
IS A MAD PIT BULLDOG
ATTACKING WITHOUT A CONSCIENCE.

His daughters had made that for his 60th birthday, after he had boasted one morning at breakfast. On another wall hung his officer's commission from the Marine Corps, Vanderbilt Law School stuff, photos of the family and friends. Among these was a big drawing of a heron (the "Government") being choked at the neck by a green frog the heron was trying to eat, with the saying, "Never give up." A fellow lawyer had made the drawing for him more than ten years ago.

He thought back. What had happened? His girls had graduated from high school, gone off and graduated from college, and were married. He now had three grandchildren.

His life had mellowed.

As a Marine ("Once a Marine, always a Marine"), he had not had any combat experience. He had become a Marine pilot and flown Douglas Skyraiders and Skyhawks in Japan, Okinawa, and Korea. All combat training exercises. Once he had tossed a nuclear bomb dummy in the wrong direction, but it didn't hurt or hit anybody.

In Hong Kong he had been arrested for fighting, and in Viet Nam, somewhere around 1959, he had bailed out into an old French cemetery and got into a deadly hand-to-hand skirmish with someone he never really saw. He lost three fingers of his left hand due to injuries in that fight, leaving only the thumb and forefinger (with limited functionality), and so he was released early from active duty.

What a night that was, he thought. It had been hot as hell, and he had regretted the day he enlisted, let alone becoming an officer and a pilot. But he had loved being called "Captain." It was a dream come true, like the amygdala defense.

This was mortal combat, too. Someone else's life was at stake, and he was responsible. At Parris Island, he had learned how to kill. As a pilot, he had learned how to drop bombs on the enemy. "Close air support," they called it. Now he would be trying to *prevent* death.

"Death-qualified" jurors normally tended toward conviction. Statistics showed they were more likely to convict on less evidence. His first job would be to stop any effort to make this a death penalty case. This was a big deal. It could mean the difference between winning and losing. Prosecutors were supposed to seek "truth and justice," but most wanted to win—just like he did. Winning was everything.

There was a knock at the door.

"Mr. Alexander."

It was his secretary, Ann. Willie's grandmother had arrived with "Mr. Green."

Ida Armstrong came in carrying a white box about the dimensions of a ream of typing paper. John had learned that she had been a schoolteacher in Mississippi before she retired to Memphis. He liked the open, intelligent look in her eyes. She seemed a proud woman. This would be interesting.

After they sat down, Ida set the box in front of her on the table, and John began.

"Did you know Willie well?"

"Yes," she said. "His mother died, and I became his mother. I took good care of him."

Alexander was struck by the coincidence. He had been reared by his grandmother not far from Memphis, in west Tennessee, Lake County, up near the Kentucky state line. He'd grown up eating catfish and hush puppies.

"My grandmother was a great cook," he said, smiling. "She cooked cornbread—'egg bread,' she called it, turnip greens, and we had pork every year when we killed hogs. Rarely had beef. We had a big garden every year."

Ida smiled. "Well, I guess we got a lot in common. Except you're white, and we're black." She waited for him to reply. They both knew what she meant.

"Ms. Armstrong, I intend to represent your grandson 110%. My being white doesn't matter. I'm color blind, but jurors aren't. We'll have trouble."

"Just excuse all the whites, Mr. Alexander," she said.

Alexander sighed. "Well, we both know it doesn't work that way." He shook his head gently. "We can't excuse people based on race, regardless of their prejudice, unless they admit it. They rarely do. But when they do, we call it 'excusing for cause.' Get it?"

She didn't. She had fought for equality all her life. She knew the odds of a fair trial were against them. Most whites in the South would not excuse that killing, whereas blacks, or African Americans, would. She wished there was no such thing as race.

Alexander, the lawyer, had already put in motion his mental wheels. They were churning. *How do I excuse whites for being white without getting caught?*

Captain Williams came in, and after Alexander had accepted the check for $100,000 and given Ida a receipt, he showed her the contract Willie would sign.

"This will be the fee agreement. Please read it. I'll get Willie to sign when he arrives. Captain Williams will pick him up at 2:00 p.m. Now, Captain Williams has lots of questions for you."

"Oh, I've got it all in this box," she said. She touched it gently. "His ribbons, citations, medals. Did you know he was a Marine officer?"

Oh, my, Alexander thought. He had assumed Willie had been an *enlisted* Marine. This was getting very interesting.

She went on. "He retired as an infantry major, 2002. Saw lots of combat. Iraq, Kuwait, the Gulf, Bosnia, Central America, in the jungles. I've got all the pictures, news clippings, everything. He was awarded the Silver Star and the Navy Cross."

Alexander was shocked again. Willie sounded so, well, black and ordinary on the telephone. Would this work *for* him or *against* him?

"Ms. Armstrong, please give Captain Williams all the details. He'll record everything for me and the trial. I'll tell you about the defense later. I also served in the Marines. I'm impressed. Major Armstrong can expect the best from me."

"Mr. Alexander, then I've just one question. Will it be the words I want to hear? Not guilty?"

"Yes, ma'am. I promise." He lied. He knew he couldn't make that promise, but why should she worry? She had just paid him $100,000. Mr. Green had arrived.

Now it was time to get serious with the defense. He called California. Helen Anderson said she would come. She understood the psychology of jurors better than anyone he knew. He had better explore the defenses of intoxication, insanity, and diminished capacity—just in case.

Accusing a man of having sex with his mother is certainly one of the greatest insults. The reaction to such an insult is usually immediate: anger and violence. This is the lawyer's classic example of what the law calls "fighting words," at least if spoken face-to-face with bad intent, as opposed to jest, or if intended for comic effect, to ridicule.

Was "nigger" just a "fighting word"? Or could Alexander convince a judge and then a jury that these circumstances, which would be shown to justify the amygdala defense, were such that he could expect a verdict of *not guilty of murder*?

Chapter 6

January 18, 2005, Tuesday
Office of John Alexander
Memphis, Tennessee
A summary of fears

Willie had decided not to fly, for fear he would be recognized and arrested. Alexander asked Captain Williams to pick him up at the bus station.

Meanwhile, two homicide detectives sat in Alexander's office. Alexander called them "Miller" and "Shorty." He pointed to an "X" under his own signature. "Now, Miller, be sure to tape-record a statement. I haven't gotten his version. I want his version fresh to you. He'll waive his rights. Here's my written waiver. Just have him sign here."

Willie arrived. Straight as an arrow he stood. He looked like a Marine, and he acted like a Marine. One hundred eighty-five pounds. As Shorty searched and handcuffed him, Alexander thought, *fighting machine.*

Dark black skin, very intense eyes. Alexander was impressed. For an alcoholic, he didn't look the part. His body language was perfect. His speech was perfect. *Let's see how he holds up under stress.*

"I haven't been talking to Willie," he said to Miller and Shorty. They didn't visibly react.

Looking at Willie, he said, "I'll be along. Get that worried look off your face. Sign the waiver, Willie. It'll be okay. Answer all their questions truthfully and directly. Got it?" He smiled.

Willie smiled back and replied, "Hey, Marine, I got it. Just do your job. I'll be fine. Get me out as soon as you can. Grandmother will post the bond. She has control of all of my money, so we're good."

After Willie and the detectives left, Alexander got busy in his office. He needed to get a bail bond set and then have Willie come back to his office. Willie's version of all this was important.

That night, Willie was still in the Shelby County Jail, but Alexander had talked to the prosecutor, Bud Jones, and they had agreed on a $150,000 bond. The judge would approve it first thing in the morning.

Alexander fell asleep only to have terrible dreams. He was in court. Willie had been convicted. The dream was about a post-conviction hearing, and there was a giant poster before the judge that read in big bold letters:

SUMMARY OF ERRORS

DEFENSE COUNSEL FAILED TO PROPERLY ASSERT DEFENSES (1) INSANITY, (2) INTOXICATION, (3) DIMINISHED CAPACITY, AND LESSER INCLUDED OFFENSES OF MURDER. ALSO, DEFENSE COUNSEL FAILED TO PROPERLY CROSS-EXAMINE THE STATE EXPERT WITNESSES AS TO THE BASIS OF THEIR OPINIONS AND MADE NUMEROUS OTHER ERRORS VIOLATING THE SIXTH AMENDMENT EFFECTIVE ASSISTANCE OF COUNSEL CLAUSE.

Oh, no!
In his dream, everyone was laughing. It was like the trial of the Knave of Hearts from *Alice in Wonderland*.
"*What?*" the judge screamed.
"The amygdala defense, your Honor."
More laughter.
The judge smirked. "You'll fry for this, Alexander. There is no such defense. *You should be electrocuted!*"
Maniacal laughter.

Alexander woke suddenly. He was in a cold sweat. His wife Lauren was talking to him. At first, he couldn't hear her.

"Get up," he finally heard her say. "Let's go to the kitchen. What's happening?"

He got out of bed.

In the kitchen, she turned the espresso machine on and watched as John Alexander, her dream come true, sat with the worst look on his face she had ever seen.

"Hey, what's wrong?" she asked, touching his arm gently. This was one of the things he loved about her.

He told her the whole story.

"The amygdala defense is the worst defense. It's never been asserted. It's a new defense. I'm the first lawyer. I'm scared. Really scared. It's like that night in the French cemetery in Viet Nam."

"Hey, Marine," she whispered. "Where's that courage like a lion?"

"Bulldog," he said. "I'm a bulldog. Devil Dog."

She smiled. He smiled. She had a way with words, and she looked as good today as she did on their honeymoon. Well, not *that* good. But he knew he was a lucky man.

He had met her on the campus at the University of Memphis. She was teaching "environmental" stuff. He was an adjunct assistant law professor. They had met by accident in a university parking lot. She had been married and was divorced. He had been married and was divorced. Both had children, and his parents and hers were deceased.

Thank God, as she used to say.

He had talked with her about his uncle, the lawyer, but rarely about his father, who had left Tennessee in 1929 during the Great Depression and moved to Washington, D.C., of all places. John was born in D.C., but his parents had soon divorced. His dad had joined the Navy in World War II and was killed aboard a ship in the battle for Okinawa.

John, along with his brother and sister, ended up in rural Lake County, Tennessee, with their grandmother, their dad's mother. Lauren loved to hear him tell his story. It was sad, but he seemed to take it in stride.

John had enlisted in the Marines right out of high school. Took a college-level GED test and was accepted at Parris Island into a program in Florida for Marine and Navy pilots. He wanted helicopters. He got what the Marines wanted: fighters and attack bombers. Lauren didn't know the difference. All she remembered was it was a "Sky Hawk" or something like that.

They had spent hours telling each other about their lives and their pains and sorrows. She had never gotten over her life as a child, and she thought his life was as sad as hers. Both had mental balloons pushed down in a muddy field that popped up from time to time.

Their honeymoon had been great. Eureka Springs, Arkansas, was what she wanted. Key West, Florida, he wanted. She won. He didn't really care. It was magic. Now, years later, the girls grown and gone, the grandkids came to visit. It was more than they could ask for. The hard times were over. Retirement was not very far away.

"Lauren," he said, "the amygdala defense. It's my last big case. I'll retire, and we'll go fishing in the Arkansas Ozarks. We'll retire there," he added, "if you want."

She listened, and she knew he meant it. She had told him it was her dream to live in the Ozark Mountains. Retirement was near. She had already quit her university teaching job and spent her time at the public library and in her garden. She had the best vegetable garden in mid-town Memphis, and she had time for her citizen-inspired environmental activities. She was president of Greener Memphis. In her mind, life was almost perfect.

"Lauren, I'm really scared," he said.

"Look, it'll work. I know you. If you think it will work, it will work."

He looked at her and knew he didn't have a choice. It would be the amygdala defense—all or nothing. All he needed was one good expert witness. Who would it be?

Chapter 7

January 20, 2005, Thursday
Shelby County Jail
Memphis, Tennessee
Justice is a game

Despite an agreement with the prosecutor, bail bond had been denied by General Sessions Judge Weldon White. But Alexander was not discouraged. He could not let the cat out of the bag prematurely, just to get bail. The defense had to remain a secret for now.

Willie had looked dejected.

In the Memphis jail, Alexander explained. "It's like playing cards or football or baseball. Justice is a game. We're not going to show them your cards until we see all of theirs or we're ready. Do you understand?"

Willie said "Yes," but he didn't. He just wanted his freedom. He wanted out of the jail.

"First things first," said Alexander. "I've got the statement you gave me at the office, and I appreciate your being honest. It's like I told you. It's a secret between you and me. It's a felony for me to reveal attorney-client secrets. I'll go to the police station and go over the statement with the investigators. I'll be right back. Just hold on." He started to get up.

But Willie couldn't wait. "Mr. Alexander, how are you going to defend me? I killed him. I've killed the enemy in combat, but never in cold blood like this. I just don't know why I did that. He said 'nigger,' and the next thing, I stabbed him."

"How long did you wait, Willie?" Alexander asked cautiously, hoping for the right answer.

"Oh, less than a second."

Alexander smiled. "That's the key, Willie. You didn't kill him, your amygdala did."

"My a-mig-di-what?" Willie looked puzzled.

"Willie, this is neurobiology. It's my field. I've studied it for thirty years. You're my first perfect neurobiological case. You see, the decision to kill came to you from your amygdala, unconsciously. The conscious part of your brain, the cerebral cortex, never activated. When he said 'nigger,' your brain lit up. Neurons activated in the amygdala, just as if he punched you square in the nose, but worse.

"Trust me, Willie, trust me. You're going to be found not guilty. We will have an honest jury. Twelve people who lay aside their fears, their misconceptions, and listen. I'll get a neurobiologist, other neuroscientists. Thank God for your money. We are going to need some more. Will your grandmother do it?"

Willie nodded his head. He was worried, but he knew Alexander was his best bet. He was back in combat again, his life on the line.

"Now, Willie, I'm sending Captain Williams over. You know he works for us. Give him a complete history of your life. I want the names of all your fellow officers and Marines—everybody, good and bad. Where you were born, and so on. Do you understand? This is important."

Willie nodded. "Mr. Alexander, money won't be a problem. My grandmother and I are worth $2.5 million. It's in a trust at Sun Trust Bank, Tampa, Florida. My brother died in Florida in an automobile accident in 2001. He lived just three months. Terrible brain injury. We got the settlement money. I want the best defense."

Chapter 8

January 20, 2005, Thursday
Office of John Alexander
Memphis, Tennessee
The molecules of his genes

While sitting in his office, Alexander was joined by his associate, Michael Benton. Alexander had met Michael in court one day, when Michael was a fairly new lawyer, just out of law school. They'd talked about Alaska. Alexander had always wanted to settle up there, and Michael had actually worked in Juneau as a fire department paramedic before he decided to return to the South and enter law school.

Michael was from Hickman, Kentucky, up on the river, and was an ardent fisherman and outdoors person. He had also operated a 30-ton salmon fishing vessel in Alaska. He was 38 when he finished law school, and he had three children. Alexander had asked him to join his firm.

Normally, Alexander didn't like associates, or even employees, and he usually worked with just a secretary and Captain Williams or another as his investigator.

But occasionally he would become interested in a new lawyer. He would bring them into the practice to try to teach them the tricks of the trade before they went out on their own. (Some of them, in turn, would teach *him*.) There were many young lawyers in Memphis who owed their start to Alexander, including some of the better defense lawyers.

"Amygdala defense. Major Armstrong. Will the judge let me argue it, Mike? Your opinion."

Alexander waited for an answer to his question.

Mike sat there, no expression on his face. He stood up and poured Alexander a strong drink of Jack Daniel's and an equally strong ten-year-old Old Charter for himself. As he

21

was pouring, he said, "I suppose you'd rather have Yukon Jack on this occasion, but I bought you a bottle of Jack, anyway." He handed the drink to John and sat back down.

"You know, John, the best time I ever had with you was when we were at Leatherwood Creek on the Buffalo in Arkansas that time you took me with your friend—what was his name? Monroe Witt? And we drank a bottle of Yukon Jack and you quoted poetry." He laughed. "I remember that story about Sam McGee from Tennessee who was burned and cremated in the stove…remember? It was so cold his buddy tore up the floor of an old boat and built a fire…."

Alexander was amused, too, and indeed, he remembered that Leatherwood Creek trip. It had been in December, cold and icy, and Leatherwood Creek was beautiful. He quietly recited some lines from the poem.

"Yet 'tain't being dead—
it's my awful dread
of the icy grave that pains;
So I want you to swear
that, foul or fair,
you'll cremate my last remains."

They both laughed.

The Leatherwood area had been great lead and zinc mining country in the old days of Arkansas. You could walk up Leatherwood Creek and crisscross back and forth over sparkling waters ankle deep. Admire the limestone bluffs, find peace and tranquility, like no other place on earth. Part of the Cherokee "Trail of Tears" was said to have crossed the Buffalo River at this point, toward a camp that would later become Yellville, Arkansas. Then it went on to Oklahoma.

Mike had been the cook that evening, over an oak and hickory fire. He'd fixed a delicious rice dish with chicken in a big Dutch oven, along with corn on the cob, baked potatoes, and an onion and tomato diced salad. The three of them had "Martha White" hush puppies, and of course, fried smallmouth bass. They liked to eat. It made the trip.

All night it had rained and rained. The creek began to rapidly rise. They had to move the boat and the tent at 1:00 a.m. It was like a flash flood. The tall trees waved back and forth, back and forth.

They were relieved when morning arrived. The 22-foot jon boat was still there, floating where their tent had been, with an anchor rope tied around a big tree.

Back to the present.

"Mike, you're one of the best lawyers I ever met. You're a mad pit bull. You've got all the talent, the intensity, the instincts to be a great lawyer, and you're one hell of a good time in the outdoors. But you're over forty. What are you going to do with your life? Do you really want to be a criminal defense lawyer all your life? You know you can make a whole lot more money with a lot less trouble handling automobile accident cases, civil litigation. You know, medical malpractice, products liability, and the like. Why don't you give it a try?"

After a short moment, as if choosing his words carefully, Mike said, "John, I'm just like you. Criminal cases intrigue me. They capture me. You're dealing with the human mind and human motives. Why did so-and-so do something—say, kill, steal, rape? Take the case I've been following in the paper—of your client from California, accused of killing the police officer. You've admitted to me that you just want to beat the death penalty. Would you mind telling me how?"

The senior partner's chest swelled.

"One of the great tricks of the trade, if you want to beat the death penalty, is to convince the jury in the first stage there is some doubt your client is guilty. Then, when they get to the second stage of the bifurcated trial, the penalty decision, if you've been successful, they'll vote for life instead of death. No juror wants to kill anybody if there is a reasonable doubt, although quite frequently they don't mind finding the person guilty. They will cheat on the guilt question, sometimes, but not on the question of punishment, if it's life or death. You see, jurors will promise you one thing and do something else. They're human. They lie and cheat just like all other humans."

Mike had heard this argument before, and as a matter of fact, he remembered it very clearly from the Leatherwood trip. This was the same argument Alexander had made with Monroe over a bottle of Yukon Jack. It was a corrupt system. All men lie, cheat, and steal. He wondered to himself if he would ever have the insight, the intellectual depth of this man he admired so much.

It was a great feeling to know John Alexander respected him as a lawyer, but he was indeed now over 40. He knew he had to make a career decision. But what he hadn't told Alexander was that he was thinking about leaving the practice of law altogether.

He had come to law school and to the practice of law wide-eyed and ready to charge, but like Alexander, he had been knocked off his charging horse the first year out of law school. He was disgusted by how much he had learned as a defense lawyer about life and humans that he didn't know before he became a lawyer.

He knew there was no justice in the system, whether for criminal or civil cases, and he just wasn't certain he wanted to continue to be a part of it—or even to fight it.

Oh, yeah, he knew lots of other lawyers around his age. He had been with Alexander to seminars and to the annual meetings of the National Association of Criminal Defense Lawyers—even one in Montreal, Canada. He had met some of the finest men on earth. As a matter of fact, criminal defense lawyers were the only group of people he knew that he really enjoyed being around, drinking with, and telling lies and tales, carousing.

He remembered that night in Montreal when they'd all stayed up until 3:00 or 4:00 a.m. and Alexander kept referring to one of the lawyers as "Doctor Bendover." He never knew why, but it was a good joke, and whenever Alexander would holler, "Doctor Bendover!" everyone would laugh or giggle.

Those were just good times. You could drink. You could sometimes cuss, tell dirty stories. One thing about criminal defense lawyers, you could sometimes be yourself. He'd said to Alexander one time, "Be yourself," and Alexander had replied, "'Be yourself' is about the worst advice you could give some folks," a quote often attributed to Mark Twain.

Alexander used another quote Mike really liked: "There are three kinds of lies: lies, damned lies, and statistics." In his *Chapters from My Autobiography*, Mark Twain had quoted and attributed the words to British prime minister Benjamin Disraeli, though the source was still a mystery. But it didn't matter who said it first, really. Alexander hated statistics, and Mike had come to know why.

Up on Leatherwood, he had heard Alexander argue that there were no theories in criminal justice that had been proven, and that the only reason to punish folks that had any possible validity was "just desserts." That seemed unscrupulous.

Monroe had acted as the devil's advocate. He had tried to quote a lot of statistics to the contrary, and Alexander had smashed his statistics. Besides, Mike knew Monroe didn't believe in those statistics, either. You could prove almost anything with an empirical study and report it in a prestigious journal, and people would accept it as gospel unless it contradicted their religious beliefs.

Mike preferred to believe, as Monroe and Alexander did, that none of the theories in criminal justice were valid.

He wondered why such a system existed. Maybe Alexander was right. It ought to be abandoned. Maybe he ought to get out and do something else.

It was getting late. Mike poured Alexander some more Jack Daniel's. The conversation continued.

"Mike, I once represented a Doctor Jayewardene. He was a gentle, nonviolent man when he came to the United States to escape the civil war in Sri Lanka. His wife was a Buddhist, and they had a ten-year-old daughter, also Buddhist. After residing in Tennessee for several years, where he was a practicing physician, they divorced.

"He was a Tamil Hindu. Many of his friends were Liberation Tigers of Tamil Eelam, who continued to fight for an independent Tamil homeland. Even the sending of thousands of troops from India did not bring an end to the guerrilla fighting. It was bloody."

Mike listened, curious.

"After his divorce, a friend in Philadelphia, Doctor Prabhakaran, who was also Tamil, arranged a second marriage for the doctor with a Hindu whom he had represented to be 'fit,' though he knew she was not. This 'friend' was having a secret, ongoing, personal, sexual relationship with her! This was a serious violation of Hindu custom and tradition. The marriage was doomed from the start.

"Soon after they were married, the woman began to refuse sexual intercourse with her new husband. Doctor Jayewardene is now wealthy and financially secure, but for months he was not able to work regularly. His income was suffering, and he was severely depressed, almost mentally ill. He talked to his lawyers and several doctor colleagues. They were all worried about his health.

"The doctor had begun to believe, upon good grounds, that there was a conspiracy between his wife, his good friend, and his wife's mother to obtain his wealth for the militant Hindus to help finance the civil war. After all, he was a millionaire. Besides, his new wife hated his ex-wife and child because they were Buddhists, and the child was never welcome in her house."

Alexander took a drink and continued the story.

"Doctor Jayewardene had purchased a very nice historic home in mid-town Memphis. Once he discovered what was going on, he employed a security guard to protect his property. After about a year of marriage, his wife announced she wanted a divorce. She filed for divorce in Tennessee.

"Then one night, she came in from a taxi ride with the 'friend,' Doctor Prabhakaran, and Doctor Jayewardene saw them in physical contact—the man's arm around her waist and his right hand touching her buttocks. He was furious. She shook her keys in his face."

Alexander raised the pitch of his voice. "'I'll be driving your Mercedes in Pennsylvania with Doctor Prabhakaran. I'm leaving tomorrow morning with my mother.'"

John had Mike's complete attention.

"The next morning at about 6:00 a.m., he took her pistol and went upstairs. The security guard he'd hired was downstairs. He doesn't remember what happened. The security guard heard shots, ran up, and found two people dead.

"The doctor had intended to kill only his wife, but he also shot the mother-in-law when she stepped into the line of fire in the small bathroom.

"The autopsy showed acid phosphate in his wife's mouth, rectum, and vagina. The doctor had not had sexual intercourse with her in over six months.

"A cab driver was located several days later who identified the wife as a woman he had picked up at the residence the day before the shooting and taken to a motel, where she met a tall Indian-looking man in a white suit and white shoes. He identified the man from a photo. It was indeed Doctor Prabhakaran.

"The cab driver had waited two hours and then returned the woman to her residence with the doctor, who accompanied her arm in arm to her front door. DNA fingerprinting matched the spermatozoa DNA of the villain doctor. It was one of the first DNA cases in the late 1980s.

"So Mike, how about it? Was Doctor Jayewardene a genetic defect?"

Mike looked puzzled. "What does genetics have to do with it? He was suffering from serious depression. I say not enough for the insanity defense. He got mad and killed her. Rightfully so. Sorry about the mother-in-law. That was a terrible accident—innocent homicide. He's liable for one killing. Manslaughter."

Mike knew jurors were unpredictable.

"Mike, what if before the shooting we could have arranged the molecules of his genes so that in that situation he would not have violated the rule, 'Thou shalt not kill'?"

"Impossible, Alexander. Impossible. You're crazy!"

Around midnight, Mike got up. "Good night, Alexander. See you tomorrow." He left Alexander sitting at his desk and went home. He knew his wife would already be angry that he was so late. If he stayed any longer, things would really be bad.

Mike Benton would become Alexander's life-long friend and the best trial lawyer he had ever met. It was his intensity, his guts. Mike was a warrior.

Chapter 9

January 20, 2005, Thursday
Office of John Alexander
Memphis, Tennessee
Kevin Newton

The office door swung open, and a heavy-set, muscular man of about six feet, two inches entered Alexander's office. He introduced himself as Kevin Newton.

"Mr. Alexander, I'm in a heap of trouble."

"Well, tell me about it, Kevin."

"I'm going to be honest with you."

"Good," said Alexander.

"I smoke marijuana, and from time to time I have sold marijuana to support my habit. I've been smoking marijuana all my life. I'm a carpenter. Don't drink much. Drink a little beer now and then. Just smoke marijuana, mostly. It makes me feel good.

"Well, the other Saturday, me and my wife, Pamela… well, we're not married, we just live together. We've lived together for 25 years. We were out hunting for antiques. We usually take a hunk of cash with us, like $10,000. She was inside, shopping at an antique store. That big one right there on Highway 51 just before you get to Covington. I was outside smoking a joint, and this guy walked up and offered to sell me 30 pounds of marijuana. Cheap. I mean real cheap, and so I bought it."

He paused, and Alexander waited for him to continue.

"You see, I usually grow my own in the Loosahatchie River bottom, but it's a lot of work. And when I had this opportunity to buy this marijuana real cheap, I took advantage of the situation. Well, on the way home we were coming

29

down the highway between Covington and Brownsville. You know the one I'm talking about?"

Alexander nodded.

"Well, we come across some state troopers, and they said it was a sobriety checkpoint and stopped us, and when I rolled down the window, the trooper asked me if I'd been smoking marijuana. And I said, 'Well, yeah.'

"He said, 'I thought so. I could smell the smoke.'

"Then he asked if I had any joints with me.

"I said, 'Yeah,' and I handed him a tin with four marijuana cigarettes in it. Well, then he looked over at my wife and said, 'What do *you* have to declare?'

"She reached in her purse and brought out six tablets. They were methadone, and she didn't have a prescription, so we knew we were in trouble. He told both of us we were under arrest and for me to give him the keys to the car, which I did, and he immediately went and unlocked the trunk and emptied all of our luggage out.

"A couple of things we had bought as antiques, and there were some boxes. Then he got down to the bottom bag, unzipped it, and lo and behold, he found my 30-pound bale of marijuana that was wrapped up in plastic. He arrested us, and here I am."

"Did you consent to the search?"

"No. What do you mean, consent? Like I told you, he just said, 'You are under arrest. Give me the keys,' and I took them out of the ignition and gave them to him. No, I didn't consent."

"Well, alright. You may have a defense here. It will be real technical. First thing, let's talk about money. Do you want me to represent you? My retainer is $10,000 cash in advance. Is that a problem?"

"No, sir. I've got a little money stashed away in a big jar in the woods. 'Ozark Bank' I call it." He laughed. "I'm from Arkansas. Hate to have to use it. We were planning to start a new house on our lot out there near Galloway. I can get the money to you by tomorrow."

"Kevin, where do you work?"

"Well, I work for the Bethen-Wilson Construction Company. They've got an office in Brownsville. There are five of us. We build houses. Three workers are illegal and alien. Mexicans."

"Do you know Mr. Graham, the new owner?"

"No, don't believe I do."

"I'm sure we will get acquainted. You get the money, come in tomorrow, and we'll get started. Your defense, incidentally, to begin with, is going to revolve around that sobriety checkpoint stop where you got arrested."

"What do you mean by that, Mr. Alexander?"

"Well, first, there are some real strict Tennessee laws on sobriety checkpoints. I will have to research that a little. And then second, I believe that the search of your vehicle without a warrant was not 'incident to lawful arrest.' That is super technical, so just leave it up to me. Get the money and come back tomorrow. How about 10:00 a.m.?"

"Fine, Mr. Alexander. You came highly recommended by Rufus Brown. Do you remember Rufus?"

"Sure do. How is he doing?"

"Well, he's been out of prison now about a year, and he's been working with me. He's kind of an assistant. He really thinks a lot of you. He says you saved his life. Calls you 'Captain Alexander.'"

Alexander grinned. "Well, we look forward to seeing you tomorrow, Kevin. I will be glad to represent you."

Chapter 10

January 21, 2005, Friday
Office of John Alexander
Memphis, Tennessee
Lies, damn lies, and statistics

The next day, sharply at 10:00 a.m., Kevin was there in the outer office with $10,000 cash. Alexander asked Ann to take the money, count it, and give Kevin a receipt, after which Kevin was to come into his office. Ann was the type of secretary who put everyone at ease.

Alexander waited in his office, thinking about the case. The arrest had occurred in Haywood County. Trial would be in Brownsville. He'd handled lots of drug cases and lots of drug conspiracy cases. He was particularly fond of Fourth Amendment cases regarding search and seizure. He believed very strongly in the Constitution, but these cases were also a way to make good money, if you were a skilled lawyer technician.

Not all criminal defense lawyers were good technicians. Lawyers had varied skills. But Alexander had worked hard at being what he called a "Fourth Amendment lawyer" and was particularly good at raising technical constitutional defenses.

Kevin came in and sat down. He got right to the point and asked Mr. Alexander what the procedure was in his defense.

"Well, Kevin, first thing I'll do is file a motion to suppress and a brief in Brownsville, and we'll get a hearing for you. Actually, you'll be arraigned. That's just you making an appearance in court and telling the judge I'm your lawyer. You'll be given a date to be back in court. Okay? Just leave it to me.

"You've given me enough information until after I have obtained what we call discovery. That is all the documents about the sobriety checkpoint, police reports, and things like that. After that, I'll let you know more about how things stand. If we win the motion to suppress, that is the end of your case, and you can go home a free man. If not, we'll talk about the alternatives."

Kevin took a deep breath, and his shoulders relaxed. Alexander continued.

"So I'll see you next in court. Get the date from my secretary as you leave. She'll call the court clerk. We have to change the date from what the state trooper gave you."

"Thanks again, Mr. Alexander," Kevin said, looking like he'd just had a huge rock lifted off his chest.

Later that afternoon, after lunch, Alexander sat in his office thinking about Kevin Newton. He figured ninety percent of all people who commit crimes don't even get arrested. Of the ten percent who get arrested, ninety percent plead guilty, and of the ten percent that don't plead guilty and therefore go to trial, ninety percent of them are found guilty by the jury.

There are lies, damn lies, and statistics. If ninety percent don't get caught, what's the use of punishing some of those who do? He knew that none of the basic principles establishing punishment for crime had ever been scientifically proven. Punishment itself was a crime.

In Kevin's case, if he didn't win the motion, Alexander thought the best thing to do would be to negotiate a guilty plea. It was just too much to ask a jury to find that he had bought 30 pounds for his own personal use.

Anyway, there was an ethical dilemma here, because Alexander already knew that Kevin had intended to sell the marijuana. Oh, he hadn't said so, but it was obvious.

But was that really an ethical dilemma?

Defense lawyers didn't have to tell the truth or argue the truth. But was it too much to expect a jury to believe this carpenter bought it for personal use?

He pondered awhile, and then the intercom buzzed.

"Mr. Alexander," Ann said, "there's a Mr. Newton on the phone. He wants to talk to you."

"Fine. I'll take it."

The line switched.

"Hello, Kevin."

"Mr. Alexander, we didn't talk about my wife's methadone charge. It's set at the same time that I'm supposed to be there, and she's charged with possession of the same marijuana, too."

"Oh, I'll handle that, Kevin. Don't worry about it. It is the same case. The fee is the same. Just have her there in court with you."

"Thank you, Mr. Alexander. Bye."

"Goodbye, Kevin."

Alexander hung up the phone. Was this a conflict of interest? Another ethical dilemma? Could he represent them both ethically?

Ethics were always getting in the way in the practice of criminal law, but that was a question he could deal with later, since she would probably plead guilty to the possession of the tablets, and he could get her a sentence with probation and probably diversion. Her record would be clean after she served a period of time on probation.

This was a good thing.

But suppose the prosecutor wants to continue to claim Kevin's wife has an interest in the 30 pounds.... He thought about it no longer than three seconds. *I'll deal with that another day.*

For the rest of the afternoon, Alexander worked in his office, polishing up his thoughts and ideas in a memorandum for the upcoming trial of Major "Willie," also known as Major William Harrison Armstrong, who had become his most interesting client.

Finally satisfied with the result, he looked at his watch. It was time to leave for his next lecture at the law school. This was his last year of teaching. He wasn't ready to quit, but he was ready to retire, to go fishing, or something.

Chapter 11

January 25, 2005, Tuesday
University of Memphis Law School
Memphis, Tennessee
Scientific defenses

"Good evening, class. Tonight we'll start with the general principles of substantive criminal law, where we left off last Thursday evening."

There were 30 students in his class, each with the desire to become a lawyer. Most of these students would become trial lawyers. "Mr. Alexander," interrupted a law student in the front row.

"Yes, Charles," Alexander said, recognizing the voice and the face as that of Charles Hoffman, one of his favorite students. The young man was promising.

"We read in *The Commercial Appeal* today about your case, William Harrison Armstrong. The paper reported that you intend to assert a new defense, 'the amygdala defense.' Could you deviate and tell us about this tonight? About this new defense?"

Alexander paused a moment, thought about it, and nodded. "Okay, we'll deviate, unless there are a substantial number of you who want to follow the outline I gave you on day one. Any hands?" No one raised a hand.

This wasn't a required course, and so most of the students had taken the course because John Alexander was teaching it. He had a reputation for being interesting and stimulating, and he was one of the best criminal defense lawyers in Memphis.

It was his practical experience that drew the attention of most of his students. He was not a "tall building" lawyer concerned only about his reputation. He was a warrior, a "bulldog," he often told them. So many teachers of law lived in ivory towers and knew nothing about the streets or the trenches of the war against crime. John Alexander had earned his reputation the hard way. He had been held in contempt a few times, criticized frequently, but he was an expert at developing the theory of the defense and all the aspects of defense of the accused. He was indeed a "Sixth Amendment lawyer."

He often told his students that to be a good criminal defense lawyer, "you never stop learning," and besides the three I's (imagination, intelligence, and industry), as he had been taught years ago in law school, he had learned that there was also a quality called "critical thinking" that was essential to success.

The goal was to become a good "Sixth Amendment defense lawyer" and then go "beyond the call of duty." The real questions, he would argue, were ethical dilemmas that defense lawyers faced daily in the trenches of the war against crime.

But now he would address another subject: scientific defenses—specifically, the amygdala defense.

"Let me begin," he said, "with a summary of the biology of the human brain and body. It is essential that as lawyers, you understand basic biological facts. You won't know what experts to hire or what questions to ask unless you have this basic understanding. Indeed, every case deserves a neurobiological approach.

"Although numbers keep changing as more information is discovered, scientists have ventured that the body is composed of up to 100 trillion cells so small that 10,000 can sit on the head of a straight pin.

"It's also said that there are up to 1,000 or more little creatures called bacteria or microbes that live on and inside your body—in your mouth, ears, nose, underarms, groin, and between your toes. They live in different parts of the body, but the majority live in your gut. Your feces can consist of up to eighty percent bacteria. And in a milliliter of human saliva live 100 million bacteria cells. Bacteria cells have no nucleus. Neither do your sex cells or blood cells.

"In fact, though mature red blood cells and cornified cells in the skin, hair, and nails must be initially formed by instructions from DNA, by maturation the DNA and the nucleus are destroyed. Though the red blood cells in blood samples don't contain DNA, there are other substances in the sample that do, such as white blood cells. Mature hair cells do not contain any nuclear DNA, and so the hair root must be used."

The students were hardly breathing. They knew they had started an exciting journey that would stimulate their imagination. Alexander had their attention.

"Now, I only have 45 minutes left of this hour, so I'd better step up the pace. As you know, the nucleus of our body cells contains 46 chromosomes—23 from Mama and 23 from Daddy. Those came from the head of Daddy's sperm cell penetrating Mama's waiting egg cell.

"Millions would be in a teaspoon of ejaculate, but only one will usually make it to the inside of the egg. Occasionally, two sperm are known to fertilize a single egg. This 'double fertilization' is thought to happen in about one percent of human conceptions.

"Chromosomes are composed of DNA—short for deoxyribonucleic acid—which is composed of four different chemicals or molecules in sequence. There are about three billion base pairs of DNA distributed over the chromosomes in the human genome. Thanks to Watson and Crick, and Rosalind Franklin, we know the chain that is formed is of two different strands twisted into a double helix. Remember your high school biology?"

Most of the students nodded.

"Now the chain or strings of DNA are composed of what has been considered mostly 'junk,' or empty space, though maybe that just means scientists don't yet know the purpose of those spaces. But about 30,000 to 120,000 sections are genes, though they are not all expressed. They use RNA as a messenger, which results in the manufacture of a specific protein or proteins for each gene. The proteins then do all the work of the body. They're synthesized in the cell outside the nucleus."

He paused, observing his students' reactions to this information. Some were taking notes, some were not, and though some seemed to already know the scope of the topic, there was interest expressed on all faces.

"So far, we know that there are more than eighty billion nerve cells in the brain. They're called neurons. In biology, whether high school or college, you should have learned all of the above, but many jurors lack that knowledge. They are scientifically ignorant, biased, and dishonest, but they will hopefully learn from your expert's testimony—a neurobiologist or other neuroscientist.

"You must weed out the jurors who do not understand this basic biology or who will not try to understand. The religious bias of the jury must not be a barrier to the amygdala defense or any other neurobiological defense. *Voir dire* means 'to speak the truth,' right? *Voir dire* will be a critical stage of the trial. Get an expert and use a questionnaire. Only one out of ten potential jurors is scientifically literate. Good luck!"

Now the students were fervently taking notes, except for a few who had degrees in biology, to whom so far, this was "old stuff."

"Now the neuron, it has dendrites, an average of five to seven of them, and some dendrites have projections on them called 'dendritic spines' that can allow for 100,000 inputs to that neuron. Electrical signals come from the senses—eyes, ears, nose, taste, and touch—to the main body or 'soma' of the cell that contains the nucleus or DNA, to the axon hillock. Then a composite signal goes down to a single axon from the soma to terminals, one to 10,000 or so. Thus, one axon transmits one electrical signal that can go to 10,000 terminals, or less, maybe one, where there are synapses or gaps to the next neuron's dendrites, or muscles, or glands. Get the picture? Let me draw a simple neuron on the board."

Alexander sketched a neuron on the blackboard.

"Now, I've oversimplified the neuron for good reason. Don't bog down here. Get the picture. The main idea. The electrical signal crosses the tiny gap, say 20 billionths of a meter, in milliseconds, via a neurotransmitter or other chemical secreted by the neurons into the gap by action of the electrical signal.

"You may be familiar with the names of some of these chemicals. There are over 100 different neurotransmitters in the brain, though only seven do the majority of the work. These include dopamine, serotonin, acetycholine, and GABA. These chemicals, these tiny molecules that are stored in the terminals, are manufactured or synthesized by the neurons, and activate, excite, or inhibit, hence the name 'neurotransmitters.' They transmit signals.

"The brain is divided into the cerebrum, the limbic system, and the brainstem. The cerebrum is divided into two hemispheres. It consists of two frontal lobes, two parietal, two occipital, and two temporal lobes. Ah, now the amygdala! Take your two fists, close the fingers over the thumbs, like this."

He placed his hands to the sides of his head. Obviously, he couldn't cover his left thumb with an incomplete set of fingers, but he wanted a symmetrical effect, and so he gave it his best shot with his forefinger and turned the right side of his body slightly toward his students so they could copy the position of his right hand.

"See? Put them beside your head, like this. These are the temporal lobes containing, like the other lobes, neurons. Millions and millions and—"

A buzzer sounded. He stopped talking and calmly looked at the class. Most continued to hold their hands to the sides of their heads.

"Our hour's up, but listen. Give me one minute to finish. If you've lowered your fists, put them back up there with your fingers over your thumbs."

He waited until they all had their fists up.

"Now lower your fists, and leaving your thumbs in your palms, open your other fingers slowly. The area at the tip of your thumb represents the area called the amygdala—a Greek word meaning 'almond' in English. It's an area shaped like an almond. There's one on the inside of each temporal lobe. This is the center of the amygdala defense."

He smiled at his students and looked forward to further clarification at their next meeting.

"See you Thursday night at 7:00 p.m. We'll continue our odyssey, and you will learn about the amygdala defense. If the neurons in the amygdala decide to kill, is the accused legally responsible? Guilty? See you Thursday night, January 27, at 7:00 p.m."

When he left his class, Alexander wondered if his students would absorb and understand his ideas, and if not, how could he ever expect ordinary citizens as jurors to understand? He would continue his lecture, but he was skeptical.

Chapter 12

January 27, 2005, Thursday
University of Memphis Law School
Memphis, Tennessee
Criteria for the defense

"It's 7:00 p.m., so let's get started. Tonight we conclude our discussion of the amygdala defense, and then we'll go back to our regular course outline. You remember in our first meeting on January 11, I said this course was divided into substantive criminal law, adjectival law, and ethical dilemmas or professional responsibility.

"'Substantive' is divided into (a) general principles and (b) the specific definition of specific crimes, such as rape, burglary, murder, and so on. 'Adjectival law' is divided into (a) evidence and (b) procedure. 'Ethical dilemmas' will be those situations defense lawyers face daily.

"We've deviated from my plan and are now considering a novel defense, the amygdala defense, out of order, so to speak. First, let's return to the amygdala itself as a structure or area of the brain."

Alexander showed the class a model of the brain.

"Notice in this model of the brain, there is no separate structure visible to the naked eye called the amygdala, like the hippocampus, which is horn-shaped and visible, or the thalamus, which is an egg-like structure and visible. It's just an area with millions and millions of neurons. The sense of smell is connected directly to the amygdala. Not so for the other senses. Where do they go? I'll return later to the senses.

"The cerebrum is covered by a thin layer called the cerebral cortex. It is only one tenth of an inch thick. A bit thicker than a credit card."

He pulled a credit card out of his pocket and held it up.

"See? The neurons are, of course, invisible to the naked eye. Six layers of neurons are in that thickness. If we counted one synapse, or connection, per second, it would take 32 million years to count all the possible connections in the cerebral cortex of one human brain! Mind boggling, isn't it?"

He paused a moment.

"This is where the decision to not commit crime ordinarily takes place—all human decisions, self-awareness, and so on. If you talk to God, it is via the cerebral cortex. And if you have free will, this is where it is located. You will find that I do not believe in free will, and that a lot of people who talk to God are actually mentally ill. That's for another day. Incidentally, never tell a jury you do not believe in free will. They will turn against you. Most citizens do not understand science."

He set the model brain to the side while he waited for the quiet murmuring to stop. He welcomed discussion and questions from his students, and these pauses offered space for their exchanges to occur. After answering a few questions, he resumed his lecture.

"Now, first the *technical* amygdala defense. It has three parts. Each part must be satisfied, or the defense fails. There will be very few cases that can meet this rigid definition, but if met, it is a complete defense and results in the words your client wants to hear: *not guilty*.

"Now, my case with Major Armstrong. Let's use that as an example. William Harrison Armstrong, a U.S. Marine, retired as a major in the Marine infantry. He served in the 4th Marine Regiment. This is a highly decorated infantry regiment made up of riflemen. The best of the best. He had retired and become an alcoholic before the day of the killing, Christmas Eve, 2004.

"Armstrong had been drinking all day at the Jack Pen, a bar on South Main near another bar called the Green Beetle. The customers are old men who, as the owner put it, think about sex and talk about sex, but do little about it.

"Incidentally, the Jack Pen is named after that pen or small barn that was used in colonial America to house a 'jack,' a donkey kept only for breeding purposes—only to breed mares—horses—to produce the then indispensable mule. But because sex is this donkey's entire world, he becomes very hostile and ornery, and he must live apart from the other animals."

Several students laughed.

"Now, back to the Jack Pen on South Main. Major Armstrong is inside the bar, talking to his Marine buddy, Bruce Voltz, a sergeant major, retired, also of the 4th Marines. Bruce and Willie have been drinking all day. They're both drunk. Major Armstrong is eating a steak, knife and fork in hand. It's just before 2:00 a.m. Snow is falling outside. It's very cold. No other customers. The woman behind the bar is the owner. The Jack Pen is open 24 hours a day, seven days a week. It's a real beer joint."

He paused to let the peaceful scene sink in. Then he spoke a little louder.

"Suddenly, without warning or explanation, Armstrong punches his steak knife into Voltz's chest, hitting his heart. Voltz had just called Armstrong, a black man, a 'nigger.' The woman behind the bar hears and sees the killing and flees out the back door as Voltz's body falls to the floor. Armstrong drops the knife, looks at the body in horror, and immediately leaves through the front door and gets into his car. He drives to Florida. Remember, in Tennessee, 'flight' is admissible evidence of guilt."

He paused again to let his students contemplate the scene. There were many different expressions on their faces, but he certainly had their attention.

"Now, let's consider what happened in relation to Armstrong's body. The amygdala can be provoked into expressing unconsciously controlled emotional responses. The amygdala can unconsciously commit a crime that the conscious person would never condone. This is not a crime of passion, in which a law-abiding and reasonable person commits a crime during a lapse of rationality or sanity. The rationale is neurological.

"The amygdala defense is not a pathological brain defense which is based upon a physical alteration in the brain. The amygdala defense is based upon the notion that the amygdala controls emotional behavior in an *unconscious* manner. The crime is committed by the amygdala *independent* of conscious thought. The amygdala controls an aggressive act, independent of conscious control, in provocative circumstances."

Alexander stopped lecturing for a moment and put up a poster he had prepared. After waiting for the students to read the poster, he slowly read the words out loud.

CRITERIA FOR THE AMYGDALA DEFENSE
in order for the defense to be established:

(1) The crime involved a relatively simple, innate, stereotyped response,

(2) executed instantaneously and

(3) without premeditation,
upon the occurrence of the provocation.

Alexander stepped away from the poster, paused, and began again.

"If the stimulus has been present for some time and consciously perceived, behavior tends to be under the control of higher thought processes, mediated by the cortex. But the kinds of responses directed by the amygdala are fast, simple, hardwired responses that are executed in a stereotyped manner or performed similarly in all members of the human species. However, if the act is deliberate, expressed relatively slowly, in seconds rather than milliseconds, involves a complex sequence of—"

A buzzer sounded. He held up his hands, palms up. He wasn't ready to stop. But he said, "That's all. We are again out of time."

He began to pack his briefcase.

All I need is an expert, he thought to himself, *to explain biology, neurobiology, and the amygdala. But where is that expert? And what about Tennessee law?*

"See you at 7:00 p.m. next Tuesday night. I'll explain why what happened is not a crime—and why Armstrong is not guilty!"

The students were unusually quiet as they left the room. None of them had ever heard of such a defense. Charles Hoffman wanted to linger and ask Alexander questions, but he knew he would have to wait until next Tuesday night. *Great course,* he thought. *Great teacher.*

Chapter 13

February 1, 2005, Tuesday
University of Memphis Law School
Memphis, Tennessee
Beyond our control

Seven o'clock p.m. Alexander was a little late. "Sorry class. I'm late. No excuse. Let's begin. The April 27, 1912, *Scientific American* included an article claiming that only one-eighth or one-ninth of the entire mass of an iceberg lies above water. Notice they were talking about mass, not height. Now, the mind or brain is like an iceberg. The conscious is the part we see, or are aware of, and the unconscious, obviously and throughout life, we are unaware of.

"We are unconscious of the operation of the amygdala. It colors memories from early childhood. It is beyond our control, whereas the cerebral cortex, the conscious brain, is within our control. There is a difference of scientific opinion as to how much control there can be and when."

Alexander rambled on, and the students busily took notes. They seemed very interested.

Finally, near the end of the hour, he said, "This leads me to mitigation evidence, the amygdala, and the neurotransmitter serotonin, but I'll leave that and other neurobiological defenses for another lecture later this semester.

"I want to remind you that your outline of the piece I assigned on Justice Thurgood Marshall is due Tuesday, March 15. I expect it on time, and I want each of you to work independently of others as you draft your view of it. I will cover this assignment in more detail later this month. Remember, the person who has the tiger by the tail is learning more than the person watching. See you Thursday."

Chapter 14

February 9, 2005, Wednesday
431 Magnolia Street
McKenzie, Tennessee
Hardy Henderson

"So you're stationed in Iraq, and your father is in the Carroll County Jail in Huntingdon for a killing in McKenzie of his wife's lover. Is his wife your mother?"

"Yes, sir."

"And you want me to represent your father? Can you handle the fee?"

The young man agreed to pay twenty thousand dollars, as a lump sum in cash. Alexander did not accept installments. Usually, if he lost, the client blamed him and refused to pay any balance due. If he won, the client said, "See there? I wasn't guilty. I don't owe you!" So it was best to collect cash fees in advance.

Alexander continued his questions.

"Excuse me, Sergeant, what is your full legal name?"

"Jay Henderson," the man replied.

"Do you have a middle name?"

"No, sir. Not that I know of."

"Well, let me ask you some questions. I see from reading the Carroll County newspaper that your father is in rather serious trouble, and I'd like to know what you know about the killing."

"Mr. Alexander, I don't know anything about the killing. I was in Iraq at the time. I got emergency leave through the Red Cross and came home as soon as I got word that this trouble had occurred. My mother has been heavily sedated and has not really told me much of anything."

"Well, all right. I don't believe there is any conflict of interest in this case. I'm certainly interested in the case, and I'm willing to represent your father, as we've agreed, so let's begin. First of all, let's you and I go to the scene of the crime. Ready?"

"Right now?"

"Of course. I've got the time, and I assume you do."

As they drove to McKenzie from Memphis, the two men chatted. Jay Henderson had quite a number of medals on his Army uniform for such a young man, and Alexander was interested in his career and his accomplishments. Henderson told him that he planned to be a twenty-year man in the Army. He'd left home at an early age because there was no work in McKenzie where he grew up, and he didn't have the money or resources to continue his education beyond high school.

"Mr. Alexander, as you know, my dad is blind, and we just really had a hard time of it. He was making brooms in Nashville. He'd ride the bus every Monday from McKenzie and come back on Friday every week. I guess that's how this trouble all got started. Anyway, you can ask him about that when we get to the jail."

"Do you know how your father lost his eyesight?"

"No, sir. I never asked him, and he never explained. It seems like he never really wanted to talk about it. We were just poor people, and my dad never really liked to talk about anything. He'd come home, sit down, get a beer, and go to sleep. That's the way I remember it."

As they drove down McKenzie's Main Street, Alexander thought to himself, *What a nice little town!* McKenzie was located in Carroll County, about 100 miles northeast of Memphis, and had been established before the Civil War after two railroads crossed at right angles. One was from Nashville headed northwest, and the other from Memphis headed northeast. The land along the Mississippi River and far inland in West Tennessee was flat farmland. Except for a few hills, it was flat as the Netherlands. Dutch European landscape paintings reminded Alexander of this Tennessee land.

There was one nine-hundred-foot hill in West Tennessee on the Tennessee River, where Confederate General Nathan Bedford Forrest's men had sunk a lot of federal gunboats by placing a cannon up on the top with which they planned to open fire on the Yankees. They had been out of range, but sure enough, the Yankees had elevated the guns on their gunboats and started firing at the impossible target. Forrest's men, when signaled, opened up with murderous fire from the brush much lower on the bank, sinking all the gunboats.

One of Alexander's great-grandfathers rode with Forrest. He was later killed at the battle of Parker's Crossroads in Carroll County.

When Alexander tired of conversation, he tried to imagine what Indian life must have been like before the Civil War. He remembered having read that there was a collection of artifacts at the University of Tennessee at Martin. He thought if he had the opportunity, he'd swing back by and visit the museum. He'd read a book written by the professor responsible for the museum collection.

Alexander's mind snapped back to reality. He was investigating a murder. "Jay," he said, "is this Magnolia Street? Do I turn here?"

"This is it. Yes, sir. Just take a right."

As they traveled down Magnolia Street, Alexander began to build an image of the neighborhood for the purposes of the defense. He saw a tree-lined street with little white houses. He imagined that whatever happened here, this man must have been trying to protect his home.

And then they were there: 431 Magnolia. It was a small and rather plain, white frame house. The killing had taken place only two days ago, and the police tape marking off the scene of the crime was still in the yard. He was greeted by a teenage daughter and some younger children. They were polite and friendly.

After introductions, he began to look about the house and grounds. After a while, he said to Henderson, "We're going to take the screen door off the front of the house, and you're going to take it to a barn on my place on Reelfoot Lake in Lake County. I'll draw you a map."

"Yes, sir."

"Do you have a vehicle?"

"Yes. I have a pickup truck."

"That's good. Let's get the door off, get it in the truck, and you take it there. I'll give you the written directions. Be sure you put it in my barn and that it's out of the weather where the rain can't hit it. Pick a spot—just look around. Then I want you to meet me in my Memphis office on Tuesday, so we can go over your testimony."

"Testimony? What do you mean?"

"Well, you're going to testify at the trial that we took this door off, and you carried it to my place in your truck."

"Why is that, Mr. Alexander?"

"I'm the lawyer. Let me do the lawyering. You be the son of the client. See the bullet holes in this door? They're at a right angle, so obviously the door was closed. These shots were fired from inside, striking the door and penetrating the wood and exiting on the outside. See these wood particles?"

"Yes, I knew that," Henderson said. "I was here when the police picked up the bullets from the yard using a metal detector. I don't remember how many there were."

"Good. That's good news. It fits my theory. We're going to visit your father now, and then I'll see you again on Tuesday."

Chapter 15

February 9, 2005, Wednesday
Carroll County Jail
Huntingdon, Tennessee
The ethics of the situation

Alexander and Jay Henderson arrived in separate vehicles at the Carroll County Jail in Huntingdon. After a short delay they were allowed inside, where for the first time he met this blind man, Hardy Henderson. The three men sat in Henderson's jail cell.

"Hardy," he said, "my name is John Alexander. I hope you've been expecting me."

"Yes, Mr. Alexander. I'm so glad you've arrived. I've been on pins and needles since this shooting occurred, and I'm glad my son was able to locate you. Does this mean you'll represent me?"

"Well, I've agreed to. I'm paid. Let's talk about the shooting. I want you to tell me what happened, and I want you to be very careful that you tell me the truth. I'm bound by whatever you say. Let me explain. If you tell me a set of facts, you can't change them later on. Do you understand?"

"Yes, sir."

"Because if you do change them, then I would have to disqualify myself from being your lawyer. Or worse than that, I may be forced to tell the prosecutor and the judge. Are you ready to tell me your version of what happened, now, knowing that you can't change it?" Alexander had lied about telling the prosecutor and the judge, but he needed the truth. If there was any lying to be done, he would do it.

"Well, yes. I suppose…." Henderson hesitated, and Alexander spoke, hoping to set the man at ease. To "prime the pump," so to speak.

52

"Well, look. Let me ask you some questions first. Did you shoot Wilbur Morris?"

"Yes, sir."

"Was he inside of your front door?"

"Yes, sir."

"How many times did you shoot him?"

"Five."

"Was this done with a .44 Magnum pistol?"

"Yes, sir. I gave it to the police."

"Did you make a statement to the police?"

"No, sir. I told them I wanted to speak to my lawyer first." Alexander was glad of this.

"Oh, that was good. That was very good. Why didn't you give them a statement?"

"Well, I don't know. But something told me I'd better talk to a lawyer first."

"Okay. Good. Now, why did you shoot Wilbur?"

"I'd rather not answer that question, Mr. Alexander. You don't have to tell the judge I didn't answer that question, do you?"

"Oh, no. It doesn't work that way. The rules of ethics are more flexible than that. In fact, our entire conversation is confidential, and it would be a felony for me to disclose anything you tell me. We're having a secret conversation. You understand that?"

Hardy was confused. It seemed to him the lawyer had contradicted himself, but he said, "Yes, sir."

"I could never disclose this conversation without your permission. Except if you try to change what you tell me."

"Well, can I get up and...can I testify....?"

"Wait a minute. You're getting the cart before the horse. How much education do you have?"

"Uh, eighth grade, sir."

"And when did you lose your eyesight? Are you totally blind?"

"Yeah, I'm totally blind. I lost my eyesight in 1968 in an accident. I was making illegal whiskey, and the still blew up. See these scars?" He touched the right side of his face and then the left.

"I see them. Well, let me ask you, Mr. Henderson. Do you love your wife?"

"Yes."

"Had she been a good wife?"

Henderson didn't answer right away, but finally he sighed and said, "Well, yes, except for this Wilbur. She had a thing going with him. You see, every Monday morning when I left McKenzie for Nashville on the Greyhound bus to work in the factory where we made brooms, she would walk me down to the bus stop on the corner and I'd leave, and I thought she went back home and, you know, did things like wash clothes and clean the house. But I learned that Wilbur would come over on Monday after I left, and he'd stay there all week. And you know, fool around."

"How do you know that?"

"My wife. She eventually told me. When I got suspicious, I told her if she didn't tell me what was going on, I'd beat the hell out of her with a broom handle and maybe kill her, and she finally, you know, confessed.

"So, last Monday when Wilbur was expected to show up, I didn't catch no bus. I was waiting at home, and I went to the door to greet him, and he must have been really surprised when he saw me, 'cause he said, 'Oh. Henderson. What're you doin' here?' And I said, 'Waitin' for you.' He said he was comin' in, and I said he wasn't comin' into my house anymore. But he did, and that's when I fired the shots."

"Now, stop, Henderson," Alexander interjected. Alexander looked at Jay and asked him to leave the jail cell for ten minutes and come back. He left.

"Now," Alexander said, "let me get something straight. Did you kill him because he was fooling around with your wife? Or did you kill him because you thought your life was in danger? You know, did you think he was going to kill you? You know, self-defense. There's a big difference."

"What's the difference?"

"Well, if you killed him in self-defense, you could expect the jury to find you not guilty and you go free, but if you killed him as a result of, you know, of his fucking your wife, well, excuse the coarse language, but that's murder."

There was a long silence.

Finally, Henderson said, "You know, I don't have much education, Mr. Alexander, but I'd like to think about this overnight before I have to answer any more questions."

Alexander said, "Fine. I'll see you in a couple of days, after I've talked with the prosecutor and Huntingdon Police Chief Reynolds. We can talk again then." They shook hands.

Jay Henderson returned and spoke briefly with his father, and then he and Alexander left the jail, returned to their vehicles, and went their respective ways.

On his way back to Memphis, Alexander decided to stop in Jackson, Tennessee, for lunch. He needed to ponder the ethics of the situation. He had just committed what he knew to be a very questionable practice. He recalled the teachings of Professor Monroe Freedman in his book, *Lawyers' Ethics in an Adversary System,* and he remembered the 1950s novel, *Anatomy of a Murder*, that became a famous movie with Jimmy Stewart and Ben Gazzara.

He knew that while Monroe Freedman had at first taught that giving the defendant the opportunity to commit such perjury was ethically acceptable, he had later decided that a lawyer that conducted himself in such a manner had committed an unpardonable sin and ethical violation. As Monroe put it, Alexander would be an outlaw, just like Robin Hood. His motives may have been good, but nevertheless he was a wrongdoer.

After lunch, as he drove along Interstate 40 trying to keep under the speed limit, Alexander kept thinking about another speech he had heard Monroe Freedman make, in which he talked about lawyers being hired guns. And then he thought of the western movie *Shane*, and he felt ashamed.

After a while, his mind wandered to the book *Crime and Punishment* by Fyodor Dostoevsky, and how the character in that book suffered and punished himself long before the crime was committed. He was now suffering from his own wrongdoing, punishing himself.

Fuck. (He hated that word.) *Punishment. What a stupid idea.* It may be valid religious theory, but he didn't believe in religion, either. And he wondered how so many people could be wrapped up in it.

He wondered how many years or centuries it would be before humans would wake up and realize that there just wasn't anything to religion. After all, if there was a Creator, he'd think a whole lot more of Alexander for being honest than he did those pious souls who showed up for church every Sunday morning and didn't believe either, but certainly were good pretenders and appeared to listen attentively— even though they couldn't remember five minutes after the sermon what the preacher had said.

About that time, he began to slow down for the Memphis city limits.

He traveled through the Memphis traffic, parallel to a railroad. An Amtrak train roared by and deafened him with its clickety-clack. Nothing like the sound of an old-fashioned train. He enjoyed that sound so much and reminisced about trains from time to time.

As the train disappeared down the track, he thought that maybe that's what would happen to religion—it would just disappear, like the train.

Hopefully, though, it wouldn't come back once it was gone. Hopefully.

Chapter 16

April 5, 2005, Tuesday
Carroll County Circuit Court
Huntingdon, Tennessee
The difference between life and death

Carroll County was created in 1821 and named in honor of Governor William Carroll. Huntingdon was the county seat. The courthouse built in 1844 was used until 1931, when it burned down. Fortunately, due to a fire-proof vault, few records were lost.

Through the stock market crash and the Great Depression of 1930, President Franklin Roosevelt attempted to help the country's economy and its people by creating agencies such as the Works Progress Administration (WPA), the Civilian Conservation Corps (CCC), and more. These New Deal programs put able-bodied but destitute men to work in public works projects, building roads, tunnels, bridges, parks, and more, thus helping them and benefiting the country.

The Neoclassical style of the new courthouse was influenced by the Lincoln Memorial in Washington, D.C., and was built by the WPA. Extensive renovations were completed in 1981. It had a long history of service.

It had now been almost two months since John Alexander had first talked with Hardy Henderson, and it was time for the Carroll County Circuit Court to meet in Huntingdon. When he appeared before Circuit Judge June Pendergast that morning and announced ready for trial, it came as no surprise to anyone. No one expected Hardy to plead guilty and spend the rest of his life in prison.

But then again, no one except Alexander knew how he was going to get out of this killing.

Alexander had brushed aside any questions of ethical dilemma he'd had, and he was ready to do battle. He could worry those ethics later in life, but for now, his job was to assert the best defense and to save Hardy's life if he could. He believed in Hardy, and he believed that he was right, even though there might be some technicalities or faults in the law.

After all, if his theories were right, Hardy's behavior was determined by genetics, and the law certainly hadn't taken biology into consideration when Tennessee and other states drafted their statutory substantive definitions of murder that would vary from state to state and depend on the rulings of various courts.

It seemed to him that murder ought to be murder, and that an innocent homicide in any state ought to have the same definition.

A few hours later, the jury had been selected, and Alexander was stuffing his papers in his briefcase. The court had recessed, and everyone had left the room except two bailiffs, Alexander, and Hardy Henderson.

"Hardy," Alexander said before he left the courthouse, "we've got a good jury, and tomorrow we'll begin the trial."

He was in his car in a matter of seconds, headed for a motel room a few miles away, and he began to think about the amygdala defense. He had this case to try first. Then he would turn his attention to getting his neurobiological experts, interviewing character witnesses, and preparing for the trial of his life.

Hardy's case was routine. It would take good lawyering, but it would be a repeat of a defense of many murders he had defended over the years. It would be a fabricated defense. He would level the playing field and seek justice according to his definition. It was situation ethics. In Willie Armstrong's case, no fabrication was necessary. He had an eye witness.

58

In this case, Hardy would have to testify, though it was his decision to testify or not.

As Alexander sat in his Huntingdon motel room that evening, looking out at a beautiful setting sun, he knew that his defense was going to have to be self-defense, focused on one juror in particular—a Sunday school teacher who, he felt, was the key to his case. It was this woman and the other jurors like her that he wanted to mold to his thinking.

His mind shifted to the case of Terrance Jackson, a young black male who'd had no social security number, no job, no address, no home, and no parents. He had defended Jackson in a case involving the murder of a Memphis liquor store owner.

The victim had owned a bar called The Midway, which was located near Alexander's home. He had gotten to know the man quite well, in a drinking man's kind of way. He had eventually lost track of him, however, only to discover years later that he had sold the bar and bought a liquor store near the same area. And then he was killed by Terrance Jackson.

The first day of that trial, the kid had shown up in his jailhouse clothing. Blue dungaree shirt, blue dungaree pants, obviously a jail uniform. Alexander was representing him by appointment of the Court. No defense lawyer would think that this was proper attire for any case that carried the death penalty.

In fact, Alexander had been one of the first lawyers in Memphis to bring about the end of trying defendants before juries in jailhouse clothes. He had also helped bring about a requirement that prisoners be served three meals a day instead of no meals a day, as often had been the case. It was enough to be awakened at four o'clock in the morning and have to sit in a cold jail cell until nine o'clock, but to do so without breakfast and to be dressed poorly, without the benefit of a shower, was disgraceful and inhumane.

Those practices had been stopped. But what he remembered most clearly about Jackson was that after he asked him if he could get some clothing brought to him, the young man had told him that there was no one to bring any clothing. He had no other clothing, no family, no relatives, no friends. Alexander had asked him if there wasn't *something*, and Jackson had simply said, "No."

Alexander nevertheless admonished the young man, who promised to be properly dressed the next day by borrowing some clothes from a cellmate. The judge, upon request of Alexander, continued the trial until the next day.

Alexander was quite distraught the next day when the jail door opened and Jackson marched into court with a beaming smile on his face, dressed in a yellow Hawaiian-style shirt with a large parrot and green and purple flowers on the front and rear! It was a shock. This was not a vacation or a holiday, and the clothing was so inappropriate that Alexander almost passed out.

He was able to easily convince the judge that the young man should be allowed to return to his cell and put on different clothes, and the case was tried the *next* day with his client wearing someone else's blue jeans and an old white dress shirt.

Just before the last witness testified, the codefendant decided to plead guilty to an agreed upon sentence of life in prison, and after a heated exchange of words between Alexander and Jackson, so did Jackson.

The proof had been terrible. The man had been executed—shot in the head by his client. The shooting was recorded by the store's surveillance video camera. Jackson claimed the pistol had accidentally fired. But the jury… what would they conclude? Thankfully, the death penalty was avoided.

Alexander never had to address in his own mind the questions of the appropriateness of the sloppy dress of that young man. Yes, the appearance of the defendant was indeed crucial, and it often made the difference between life and death. Just another flaw in the system.

Alexander always wore the finest clothes he could buy, with a Western-style cut, large ties, cowboy hat, and as much color in his tie as good taste would permit. He wanted to look different, and he wanted the jury to know that he was the defense lawyer whenever he stepped into the courtroom.

He tried to avoid looking like a prosecutor, and he never wore the kind of clothes that a banker would wear, with lots of stripes in gray or black. Instead, he wore light-colored clothing that got even lighter in color as the trial progressed. Many times, he wore his white linen suit, although many lawyers thought that such a suit was in bad taste. He wanted to be sure he was different and that the jury knew it. He was the White Knight.

Exhausted, Alexander undressed and stretched out on the motel bed to think not about Terrance Jackson, but about Hardy Henderson's defense. The large overhead fan gently rotated, stirring the air in the room just enough to make it comfortable. Then he was asleep.

Lightning flashed and struck, and he could see the face of a witch doctor, an ancient Indian witch doctor who was explaining to a handful of tribesmen that God was angry and that the lightning was His expression of anger. He thought, even in his dream, how foolish were the explanations of men for that which they didn't understand. The lightning flashed and flashed, and finally a giant bolt struck the witch doctor and the tribesmen disappeared.

Alexander jerked awake in bed and realized he had only been dreaming. He fell back and went to sleep again.

Chapter 17

April 6, 2005, Wednesday
Carroll County Circuit Court
Huntingdon, Tennessee
Leaving well enough alone

It was the day of the trial. The jurors were sworn in, and Judge June Pendergast warned them, quite properly, as to their duty. The prosecutor, Frederick Schultz, began calling witnesses, the first being Police Chief Reynolds, who had arrived first on the scene.

"Chief Reynolds," he asked, "did you take this pistol from the hand of Hardy Henderson, the defendant, seated in the chair there beside Mr. Alexander, when you arrived at 431 Magnolia on the seventh of February?"

"Yes, sir."

"Let it be marked Exhibit One."

The clerk took the pistol, a Ruger .44 Magnum, and handed it to the court reporter, who fastened a tag around it and marked it Exhibit One.

Alexander stood.

"No objections, of course, Your Honor," he said as the exhibit was being marked. He was dressed in a charcoal brown suit with a red United States Marine Corps tie that featured a bulldog emblem with a World War II Marine helmet. He might wear his white linen suit for final argument, depending on the weather. He smiled at the jury as he sat back down.

The prosecutor continued. "And are these the bullets that you personally recovered, with the assistance of your men, in the front yard and street that same day? These five bullets you see here?"

"Yes, sir."

"And would you show and explain to us this diagram that you have prepared?"

Here, the judge interjected. Looking over at Alexander, she asked, "Any objection, Mr. Alexander?"

"No." Alexander smiled again, looking over at the jury.

"Proceed," said the judge.

The prosecutor continued. "And is this the diagram you have personally prepared, showing exactly where the bullets were found and their distance from the front door of 431 Magnolia?"

"Yes, sir. I'll be glad to explain."

"Proceed."

Alexander sat there, thinking perhaps he should ask no questions of this witness. He had determined that Chief Reynolds was a friend of Hardy's, as revealed by his investigation of Hardy. His testimony should be favorable. Reynolds' diagram of where the bullets were found supported Alexander's theory of the defense.

But when the prosecutor concluded, Alexander said to Judge Pendergast, "Your Honor, I have just a few questions."

He walked over to the chief and positioned himself so the jury could see both of them clearly. He began.

"Chief, when you arrived on the scene, did you notice the front door? A screen door?"

"Yes, there was a screen door."

"And did you notice whether there were any bullet holes in that screen door?"

"Yes, as a matter of fact, I did notice the bullet holes, but I didn't remove the screen door. I left it there. I understand it's been removed, and as a matter of fact, I've been told that you have the screen door, Mr. Alexander."

The prosecutor shifted his eyes and glared at Alexander. Alexander had not revealed that he had the screen door.

"Well, I want to ask you another question, Chief," Alexander continued. "Did you take a statement from Mr. Henderson when you arrived on the scene?"

"No, sir."

"Did he refuse to answer any of your questions?"

"No, sir, I didn't ask him any questions. I thought he ought to talk to his lawyer first."

"But at any time did he refuse to answer any questions?"

"No, sir."

"You did not ask him why he shot the deceased, Wilbur Miller, did you?"

"No, sir."

"This home, 431 Magnolia, is the property of Hardy Henderson. You know that. It's his home. He lives there with his wife?"

"Yes, sir, that is correct. I've known Hardy Henderson for more than twenty years, and that's where they've lived."

"And you knew that he was blind, totally blind?"

"Yes, sir, I knew that."

"And you knew that he works in a broom factory in Nashville and travels there each Monday?"

"Yes, sir."

"On that particular Monday, did you ask him why he did not go to work?"

"No, sir. I didn't ask him any questions."

"No further questions, Your Honor."

The next witness was called by the prosecutor. "Doctor Jerry Benson." Benson approached the stand, was sworn in, and began his testimony.

The prosecutor established the credentials of the doctor as a medical doctor and physician in good standing, having practiced in McKenzie for many years. Alexander happened to know the doctor and remembered the only other case he'd had with him.

The doctor had testified in his favor that a customer of a bootlegger had died of natural causes, and that an autopsy had revealed there was no evidence of criminal homicide. Alexander liked the doctor and felt that he was fair and wouldn't cheat. He had known other doctors to cheat for the prosecution. This doctor was not one of them but one of a rare breed.

As he recalled, the bootlegger had slapped the customer after an argument over a five-dollar indebtedness, and the man had collapsed on his front porch, dead. The bootlegger had fled down the railroad track and eventually hitchhiked to Memphis and then to Alexander's office. He remembered the case well because of the bizarre circumstances of the bootlegger running down the railroad tracks.

In any event, Doctor Benson didn't know about the slapping and was basing his medical examination on the physical condition of the body that was examined. He said it was an embolism or a bubble in the brain capillary that had burst, and there was no evidence of trauma. He could not, therefore, support any criminal agency theory, and Alexander's client was never indicted.

Alexander had backed prosecutors down before, but that was the only case he could remember, other than one in Martin, Tennessee, that involved a marijuana transaction where the police had set the trap too soon, and his client had been caught with no money or marijuana. With just a little bit of bullying and a threat to win published in the newspapers, the prosecutor had declined to indict.

Now, here he was with Dr. Benson again, and he would have to gamble.

"No further questions," the prosecutor concluded, having shown the cause of death to be the gunshot wounds. He was smiling as he sat down, and he looked toward Alexander as if thinking, *What can you possibly do to this witness to help the defense?*

"Good morning, Doctor Benson. I'm John Alexander. You remember me?"

"Yes, sir. Good to see you again."

"I'd like to ask you a few questions on behalf of the defense, for the benefit of the jury." He smiled and glanced at the Sunday school teacher, whose eyes were glued upon him in obvious rapture. He then wheeled around and began with a series of questions about the exact location of the wounds on the body, their entry and exit points.

"Now, would it be fair to say, based on the testimony that you've just given, Doctor Benson, that all of the gunshots entered from the top of the head or face and were in a slightly downward motion, as if to say the deceased was facing the line of fire and that the head and body of the deceased was lower than the point where the bullets were exiting the .44 caliber pistol? And you've seen the pistol introduced in this case as the weapon used in the killing?"

"Yes, I have, and I would say that that's a fair summary of my opinion."

"Thank you, doctor. One final question. This bullet wound here on the top of the head, exiting downward. Can you say whether it was the first or last shot?"

"Well, in my opinion—and I don't think I'd be speculating here—that would have been the last shot fired in the series. The exit wounds took most of the back of his head."

Alexander wanted to ask *why*, but he decided to leave well enough alone and hoped that the prosecutor would not attempt to clarify that point. It was the exact testimony he wanted, and once again Benson had been fair. Really, more than fair. What a strange doctor. Alexander wondered how he kept his position as coroner and medical examiner. Most prosecutors would have gotten rid of such an honest doctor.

At this point, the court took a recess for the day. While the jurors were filing out, Alexander was beginning to feel more comfortable with the case, the Huntingdon courthouse, and the jury. The judge, too. She had been gracious, and the testimony was fitting into his puzzle exactly as he had hoped or planned.

As soon as the jury had cleared the room, Alexander motioned to the bailiff to allow him and his client to be escorted out the side door of the courtroom to the jail area. Now the remaining piece was the testimony of his client.

Should his client testify? He knew this was a decision that only the client could make, because under the system of criminal jurisprudence practiced in the United States, the client makes three decisions: what plea to enter (guilty or not guilty), whether to testify or not testify, and whether to appeal. All the other decisions were to be made as tactics by the criminal defense lawyer, keeping the client informed, of course.

After they had left the courtroom and were seated in the back room, Alexander began by saying, "Hardy, you must decide whether you are going to testify or not."

"What do you think, Mr. Alexander?"

"Well, Hardy, of course it's your decision, but I will certainly try to give you the best information I can to help you make that decision. You've heard the testimony, and I think it fits with what you've told me. The doctor has described the gunshot wounds, which physically fit the description you've related to me of the event. And of course, we have the door.

"Why don't you think about it tonight, and you can let me know first thing in the morning. I'll be prepared to go either way. We'll postpone the case until tomorrow. I'm sure the judge will do that."

"Sure, Mr. Alexander. But I want you to know now—I want to testify."

"I understand. But what you may not understand is that in most cases that is the worst thing a defendant can do, because it opens you up to cross-examination."

"What do you mean?"

"Well, I've explained this to you before. They get to ask you about all sorts of things. And you know that if the prosecutor asks you about your blindness, you've got a problem."

"Well, I can tell him like I told you—that it was a whiskey still explosion."

"Yes, but you've also confided in me that you were in prison for armed robbery at the time you were making the whiskey secretly in prison."

"I see. He's going to ask me about the armed robbery conviction, isn't he?"

"No. He didn't disclose that to me pretrial, and for some reason or another I think he's overlooked it. Unless you accidentally or voluntarily bring out that you were in prison, it shouldn't get into the evidence. I don't think he knows you've been in prison. So it's a tough decision, just as I've said over and over again, and I'm going over it with you again. Do you understand?"

"Yes, sir. But I want to take that chance, that risk."

"Well, think about it overnight. I'll be prepared to go either way, and you can let me know at nine-thirty tomorrow morning. Goodnight, Hardy."

As Alexander had hoped, the case was continued to begin at 9:30 a.m. the next day.

That night, Alexander didn't sleep. He knew that this was a two-edged sword, and he knew that if the jury heard about the armed robbery conviction, Hardy could very well be in trouble. On the other hand, if he testified successfully, and the armed robbery conviction was not disclosed, it would certainly make out clearly his case of self-defense or defense of habitation—and with the judge's charge, under the law of Tennessee, the jury should return a verdict of not guilty.

There shouldn't be even a question of doubt. The man would make a good witness—as long as the armed robbery conviction didn't get into the evidence.

Chapter 18

April 7, 2005, Thursday
Carroll County Circuit Court
Huntingdon, Tennessee
A man's home is his castle

The next morning at 9:30, Hardy was sitting in his chair behind the defense lawyer's table.

Alexander arrived, trim and dapper, wearing the white suit that had become his trademark. It was a warm April day, and the sun was shining brightly. His graying beard was briskly combed, his hair cut short like a Marine. He wore glasses, as his eyesight was now very poor, and of course, there was his disfigured left hand, which was always visible.

Lots of folks wondered why he didn't do something to cover that hand, but Alexander always said, quite candidly, that letting it show gave him a certain edge on his adversary. Judges and jurors seemed to feel some pain or anguish, some sensitivity toward him, and like any good lawyer, he knew to capitalize on the feelings of his audience.

After all, the injury had occurred when he was a Marine in defense of his country, and there was no patriotism greater or equal to the duty to defend one's country—except jury service, as he often told juries, and as he intended to tell this jury in particular.

"Good morning, Hardy. Have you made your decision?"

"Yes, sir. I want to testify."

"All right. As soon as the judge gets here and we get started, I'm going to call your son. Then I'll call you. He's in his Army uniform and looks great."

In a few moments, Judge June Pendergast entered the room in a crimson red robe, and the court was called to order by the bailiff, who began, "Oyez, oyez!" Everyone stood.

After the judge's formal entrance, everyone was seated and trial was set to continue. Judge Pendergast looked at the prosecutor and said, "Let us resume the testimony."

He replied, "Your Honor, we rest."

Alexander had expected that Schultz had no other witnesses or proof, and he was ready with his motions, which were routinely made and denied by Her Honor as he expected. Trial judges rarely ever granted motions to dismiss charges at the conclusion of the State's case, particularly in murder cases.

The judge was an ex-prosecutor and very conservative. She always denied *all* defense motions. She had recently boasted in a private meeting at the Carroll County Golf and Country Club that no defense lawyer would claim she ruled in their favor.

This was a jury question and a case the judge ought not take from the jury, which Alexander knew, despite her bias. "Your Honor," he said, "in view of the denial of our motions, we are ready to proceed with the defense. I'd like to advise Your Honor that my client will testify and that I have one other witness that I'd like to call at this time."

"Proceed, Mr. Alexander."

"I call Jay Henderson."

Into the courtroom walked a young man with a clean, crisp, green U.S. Army uniform—his left breast covered with medals and ribbons. He was a handsome sight, and Alexander knew that this was part of the art of being a defense lawyer. Although he despised the system, he had become a master of the trade. This wasn't a profession, and it wasn't just a business. It was more. It was a show, and it was showtime.

"Mr. Henderson, state your full name, occupation, and place of residence."

"Sergeant Jay Henderson, United States Army, stationed in Iraq."

The eyes of everyone in the courtroom were fixed upon the witness. Alexander moved quickly to his left and took up a position behind the jury box so the jurors could not see him but would continue to focus their attention on the young witness.

"Sergeant Henderson, on Wednesday, the ninth of February this year, did you and I go upon the premises in McKenzie known as 431 Magnolia?"

"Yes, sir."

"And was this premises known as your home and that of your father, Mr. Hardy Henderson, seated to my left?"

"Yes, sir."

"And this was your home—your castle, so to speak?"

"Yes, sir, except that I have been serving in the Army in Iraq. The Army is my career."

"But this is where you grew up and where you lived with your mother and father until you graduated from McKenzie High School and left, correct?"

"Yes, sir. It's the only place we ever lived. It belonged to my grandfather Henderson before he died."

"Let me hand you a photograph of that house. Is this an accurate photograph of the house, showing the oak trees there in the yard?"

"Yes, sir."

"Your Honor, we ask that this be marked as defense Exhibit One."

The exhibit was marked by the court reporter.

"And did we remove the screen door from the house, you and I?"

"Yes, sir."

"And what did you do with the screen door?"

"I put it in my Dodge pickup truck and took it to your barn in Lake County on Reelfoot Lake."

"All right. That was approximately two months ago. And what next did you do with the screen door?"

"I picked it up yesterday at your instruction, and I've got it with me. I brought it over with me in my truck. It's out in the hall."

"Your Honor, at this time we'd like to bring in the screen door."

"Your Honor, we object," said Schultz. "The discovery rules…."

"Your Honor," countered Alexander. "It's relevant. It contains the bullet holes with respect to the firearm that was discharged in this case." He looked over at the prosecutor. "He knew that."

"Objection overruled. Bring in the door."

Alexander was shocked. He had expected a heated argument and ruling. Judge Pendergast didn't have any trouble with that objection. Why was she so easy on this one? This was not her reputation.

The door was brought into the courtroom and marked as an exhibit, and at Alexander's request, each of the jurors was allowed to examine it.

The prosecutor asked no questions, not really knowing what had happened to him. He felt Alexander was taking the case away from him and was building the defense—the best defense. "That's all I have, Your Honor," Schultz said. "Pass the witness."

Alexander sat down, still puzzled. The judge must be planning something awful for him. He strained his imagination. No clue.

Alexander continued. "Your Honor, I call the defendant, Hardy Henderson."

Mr. Henderson stood up, white cane in hand, and the bailiff stepped forward and assisted him to the stand. All the jurors' eyes were riveted on Hardy's every step.

Alexander began. "Mr. Henderson, please state your full name, occupation, and address."

"Hardy Henderson, 431 Magnolia, McKenzie, and I'm a broom maker in Nashville. I go there about 100 miles by Greyhound bus each Monday and return home each Friday. We have quarters there in the broom factory, where we live during the week."

"Mr. Henderson, I see that you have a cane, and it's obvious, but would you state to the jury whether you have any eyesight?"

"I'm totally blind and have been since 1968."

Alexander winced to himself, as he knew this was getting dangerously close to opening the door to that armed robbery conviction. Hopefully, the prosecutor had not done his homework.

"All right now, Mr. Henderson, would you just tell us what happened the day of the shooting? But first of all, let me ask you a question. You are married to Shirley Henderson, and the young man that just testified is one of your children. Is that correct?"

"Yes, sir."

"And he graduated from high school and left home. Just you and your wife live there at 431 Magnolia?"

"Yes, sir."

"And you've been married for 32 years. Is that correct?"

"Yes, sir."

"All right, now. Tell us just what happened."

"Well, I was at home that morning. Ordinarily I would catch the bus at the Log Cabin Restaurant down the street, on the corner, and Shirley would walk me over there, but we had a disagreement and I decided to stay home that week. When someone knocked at the door that morning, I didn't know who it was, but I had my pistol.

"I'd heard some dogs barking, and I was afraid of burglars. In fact, I'd been awake since three o'clock that morning. My son Jay had bought me the pistol, you know, for protection. Even though I was blind, he taught me how to use it. You know, by going by the sounds, shooting at the sounds."

He paused for just a moment and then continued.

"Well, I went to the door, and Wilbur Miller was there. I knew it was him, and I knew that he'd been fooling around with my wife. In fact, that's what we'd had the disagreement about. I told him that he couldn't come in and that he wasn't welcome in my house anymore, and he was not to come back.

"Well, I heard the door open, and I said, 'Wilbur, I told you not to come in.' And then I felt Wilbur's hand around my neck, and he was shouting, 'Hardy, I'm going to kill you, you son of a bitch!'" He had everyone's attention.

"I'll just never forget those words, because I was scared. I didn't expect that. He was squeezing my throat. It felt like he was choking me. I had my pistol, and I backed away quickly. I mean, I felt like, it seemed like, he was coming toward me, although he didn't have his hand on my neck anymore, and I shot and I shot and I shot and I shot! I heard him hit the floor, but before that his face came down on my shirt, and I could feel the blood on my shirt with my hand."

"No further questions, Your Honor," said Alexander. He thought to himself, *Well done. Now let's see if the prosecutor has done his homework.*

The assistant prosecutor, Billy Jordan, stood up and began to question Hardy. He asked question after question designed to confuse him, but Hardy told his story over and over again. Alexander kept thinking about those bullet holes in that door and the bullet holes in that head, and the testimony matched over and over. Frustrated, the assistant prosecutor sat down and concluded by saying, "No further questions, Your Honor."

Alexander looked at Henderson and wished the man could see—that he could look into his eyes and silently say, "We've been lucky. We made it." But he knew that

Hardy, moving step by step across the courtroom with the aid of his cane and the bailiff, knew exactly where he stood, despite a limited eighth-grade education. The jury had watched every step.

Alexander's closing argument was great, one that he would always remember—and perhaps one of the easiest that he'd ever made. With that Sunday school teacher juror sitting there, he was able to effectively paint the picture of that little white frame house with those two big oak trees on Magnolia Street.

"A man's home is his castle," he had argued. "That young son serving his country in Iraq, that front door with those bullet holes at a right angle going from inside to out. Hardy had been inside his castle. A man's home is his castle, no matter how frail. The winds may blow, the rains may come in, but it's still his castle and his home. And when another man threatens to kill that man, especially a blind man, he certainly has a right to fear those threats and to believe that his life is in danger. Any man would have done exactly what Hardy did."

Early on in the argument, when Alexander had argued "a man's home is his castle," the school teacher had begun to cry. And there were tears in the eyes of other jurors. Alexander knew that he was going to win this one.

The prosecutor tried to paint a vivid case of first-degree murder, to no avail.

The jury was out fifty-five minutes before it returned with a verdict of "not guilty," ending the trial. It had been simple. The best defense is a simple defense.

Alexander felt relieved and excited.

On his way home that evening, he thought about an old lawyer he had known from Ash Flat, over in Sharp County, Arkansas. He recalled the old lawyer's tale about the young boy who had come into his office there in Ash Flat and had said, "Mr. England, I need you to represent me in a burglary case."

"Well, son," the lawyer had said, "what are you accused of burglarizing?"

"Well, they say I burglarized a gasoline station. You know, the one down by the Dairy Queen."

"Well, what's the evidence?"

He said, "Well, they had my cigarette lighter with my initials on it."

"Well, son, you must have dropped that earlier that day when you were in there to buy gas. Didn't you? Isn't that what happened?"

The boy looked puzzled, and then he grinned and said, "Yes, sir, that's right. I was in there earlier that day buying some gas and dropped my cigarette lighter."

"Well, if that's the only evidence they have, we can explain that. They didn't catch you inside, so it seems to me like there's no case."

Alexander would never forget the dilemma, the trilemma, with which he had been faced in defending Hardy Henderson, nor its resolution. He was certain that justice had been done, although truth may have suffered. Hardy Henderson was a free man again. But they had fabricated a defense. Hardy shot, not in self-defense, but to kill his wife's lover.

Alexander didn't feel guilty. He didn't care. It was time to return to the amygdala defense and Major William Harrison Armstrong, USMC. He wouldn't have to fabricate Armstrong's defense.

But Alexander couldn't possibly know what the future had in store.

Chapter 19

April 13, 2005, Wednesday
West Tennessee Detention Facility
Mason, Tennessee
Harry Prince

It was late, and Alexander was at home asleep when he was awakened by a telephone call. "Mr. Alexander, this is your answering service. We have a telephone call for you. The woman said it was urgent."

"Give me the number. I'll return the call." He took the number, wrote it down on his pad, and at first thought that at his age he should just ignore the call. But he dialed the number and waited. It rang once, and a panicked female voice answered, saying, "Hello, hello!" barely above a whisper.

The whisper caught him off guard, but he replied quickly, saying, "This is John Alexander returning your call. Is it something urgent?"

"Yes, Mr. Alexander. I'm Judy Prince. You've got to come immediately. My husband Harry has been arrested and is being taken to the federal detention facility at Mason."

"What happened? Can you tell me any other details?"

"Well, he's accused of being a drug dealer. They say he had an airplane and was flying in marijuana in large quantities from the Caribbean. Can you come quickly? This is urgent."

"Well, ordinarily I don't do that, but if you insist.... It's 2:00 a.m. Of course you know this kind of service is expensive. Lawyers charge large fees."

"Mr. Alexander, I know you. I know your reputation. I'm prepared to pay you ten thousand dollars cash when you get here."

"Well, I would prefer a cashier's check," he lied, "but we can take care of that after I arrive. Give me your address,

78

your number, and your husband's name, and let me meet you in Mason. We'll go visit him together."

"Fine," she said, her voice seeming to regain some strength. "I'll meet you at the gas station in Mason where the highways cross. Okay?"

"Yes," he said. "In two hours."

The conversation was over, and Alexander was out of bed getting dressed. He wondered how much longer he was going to be able to do this. He was feeling very old, but he hadn't retired yet, and this case did sound interesting.

On the way to Mason, he drove as fast as he could, often breaking the speed limit by a few miles. He didn't want to get stopped and get a ticket or be delayed, so he held it as close as he could to fifty-five or sixty-five, depending on the speed limit. He never did appreciate speed limits. He thought about the German Autobahn and how people reportedly drove at outrageous speeds. He wondered about the statistics on speeding and what the real truth was about automobile accidents and speeding. Like drinking and speeding.

He never did think that just because you had something to drink and were in an accident that it was caused by the alcohol, as was claimed by prosecutors and "Mothers Against Drunk Drivers" and other such outrageous organizations.

Well, anyway, he hadn't had anything to drink for several days, so he didn't have to worry about a DUI charge as he raced along the highway in pitch darkness except for his headlights. There was almost no traffic.

Soon he was in Mason, and he met Mrs. Prince at the corner gas station, where she had assured him that she would have his cash. She had it.

He quickly said, "Let me hold the money, if you don't mind, and we'll convert it to a cashier's check as soon as the bank opens in the morning."

"I understand, Mr. Alexander. I've hired lawyers before, and I know how you think."

"Yes, we want to get paid. And when we've been paid, there's no question that our minds work better." He grinned. He liked this woman, and he listened to her story.

She was ordinary. A waitress, she said, working most of her life until she met her husband, who was much older. They didn't have any children, and neither had been married before. They had married and settled down.

She had absolutely no suspicions or idea that he was engaged in any illegal business and denied that could possibly be true, but Alexander pointed out that she was not with her husband at all times. She admitted this, saying that he had been a farmer, "rice and that sort of thing, you know," and had a considerable investment in chickens and turkeys.

"Well," Alexander said, "let's go to the federal jail and see what we have."

At the federal jail, he was greeted by several officers who at 4:30 a.m. did not want to make the arrangements to allow him to enter—until he threatened to call a judge and pointed out the seriousness of denying a person access to his attorney, despite the hour. Finally the arrangement was made, and he was in a room with Mr. Harry Prince. Mrs. Prince was required to remain in the parking lot in her car.

Mr. Prince was in his fifties and very sure of himself, although quite disturbed at the way he had been handled.

"Mr. Prince, I know it is quite upsetting and a shock to you to be sitting here, but it's important that I ask you some questions and get good answers. Your wife has hired me. Do you mind talking at this time in some detail?"

"No, I understand, Mr. Alexander. We know about you. We heard about you when you represented those folks in the horse race scandal, and we heard about your Little Rock coal fraud case, so I have a lot of confidence in you, and I'm willing to answer any questions you have."

"Well, first of all, you're accused of illegally importing marijuana, I understand a federal charge. Do you know the agents who arrested you?"

"Well, there was this FBI agent named Scotty Boomershine, and Eddie Gregory was the other. They were pretty rough. Tore our place up. I wasn't even dressed when they dragged me out of bed, and I really don't know what this is all about. They tried to get me to make a statement that said that I had an airplane and had been importing marijuana in large quantities from the Caribbean, and they said something about Quaaludes and cocaine, which is all nonsense.

"I've made my money in the farming business, although I'll admit to you, Mr. Alexander, in the old days I did a little bootlegging around the university when I was a student. I didn't graduate, by the way. I had to come home. My father died, and I had to take over our Arkansas farm. And I've done rather well."

"What do you say you're worth in dollars and cents?"

"Well, it'd be several million."

Alexander began to realize that he needed to adjust his fee upward.

"And you're saying that all this property and money you have can be traced legitimately?"

"Certainly it can be traced. Yes, the chickens, the turkeys, the farmland—and I've got about one hundred American Quarter Horses. We have one of the best Quarter Horse ranches. It's here in Tennessee. If you read any of the horse magazines, you'll see I'm listed in the top ten. You know, for breeding and showing, that sort of thing. Do you know anything about horses, Mr. Alexander?"

"Not really, Mr. Prince, but we can get to that later and you can educate me. Let me get hold of the FBI agents in this case and see what we can do. I'll talk with you in the morning. I'm quite certain you'll be brought before a U.S. magistrate and taken to Memphis. Do you understand that?"

"Yes, sir."

"We'll get a bond set for you and get you out as soon as we can."

Later that morning in Memphis, a ten thousand dollar cashier's check in his pocket, Alexander was standing outside the magistrate's chambers waiting for the proceedings to begin when he recognized agents Boomershine and Gregory. He'd known them from several encounters before, and neither liked him very much. In fact, he didn't like them, either.

He didn't really like any FBI agents. He thought they were the worst law enforcement agency around. Oh, it wasn't that they couldn't develop cases and didn't do a good job; it was because the entire federal law enforcement system, including particularly the FBI, was based on a system of snitches or cooperating individuals, and he didn't have any use for any such system.

The idea that we would have a criminal justice system based on such a concept, perfected by the Nazi Germans and their Gestapo in their persecution of the Jews, Gypsies, Serbs, and others, sickened him. He was sure Hitler's *Mein Kampf* had become the bible for law enforcement in the entire western world!

He didn't think the system the FBI developed was a moral system of law enforcement, but he knew not to cross the FBI, the DEA, or the IRS. It was important that you didn't get any of these agencies on your tail, not to mention local law enforcement. There just wasn't anything he liked about the criminal justice system, and society certainly needed an alternative, he thought.

About that time, his thoughts were interrupted by the entrance of Magistrate Charlotte Montpier. She was a good magistrate and had always been fair to him, although he didn't really trust any judge or magistrate in the system. He continued to think that everybody was a cheater and that they operated under the theory that "the end justifies the means."

The bail bond was set, and his client was released. The federal train had begun its journey, but it would be months before a jury trial. A negotiated plea would be impossible.

Chapter 20

April 15, 2005, Friday
Office of John Alexander
Memphis, Tennessee
An excellent witness

Alexander had again been distracted from Armstrong's amygdala defense. It had been months since he had been hired to defend Major Armstrong. He would have his investigator immediately line up the character witnesses for interviewing. He had taken another new case. This would have to be his last. It was time to retire.

He would contact Doug Booth, the chief neuroscientist at the University of Tennessee research labs in Memphis, to see who he would recommend as witnesses. Doug was an excellent researcher and teacher.

Next, he knew a Ph.D. molecular neurobiologist who lived in Texas, Dr. James Barrow. Dr. Barrow's wife was from Mexico, and because it suited her better to be closer to home, he had left Vanderbilt University in Nashville for a better job at the University of Texas, El Paso.

While Dr. Barrow was still at Vanderbilt, Alexander had hired him to testify in a murder case involving the neurotransmitter serotonin. He had lost that case, and his client had been sentenced to death, but the case was on appeal a third time, and another lawyer had taken over.

Alexander shuddered at the thought that the defendant might be executed. Actually, he had been appointed to represent the defendant ("Cat" Stevens) *after* he had been found guilty, sentenced to death, and the case was remanded for a new sentencing hearing only. He had not been able to attack the jury's finding of guilty of murder. The only issue had to be with the sentence: life or death.

Alexander had introduced expert opinion testimony or evidence in mitigation, to get Stevens life in prison as opposed to the death penalty. Dr. Barrow had been an excellent witness. Fluid from spinal taps at L2 in the lumbar spine of the defendant Stevens were analyzed at the Vanderbilt University lab in Nashville, where Stevens was now on death row. This analysis established that Stevens had the lowest level of serotonin ever scientifically established. The prosecutors offered no evidence in rebuttal.

As a molecular neurobiologist, Dr. Barrow had testified for the defense that Stevens had no control over his impulse to kill. He had killed a 79-year-old woman by stabbing her in the chest in a parking garage after she had called him "son." He had cut her purse and snatched it, and when she had said, "Son, why did you do that?" as he turned to flee, Stevens turned and stabbed her to death.

Dr. Greenfield, a Nashville psychiatrist, testified that Stevens was abused as an infant by his mother before she abandoned him at the age of one, after which he was adopted by another woman whose husband sexually abused him.

Abandoned, adopted, and abused. All recorded in his memory, colored by his amygdala and hippocampus. Alexander wished he could have asserted the amygdala defense in that case, but all he could do because of the law and the judge's rulings was to use the evidence to mitigate against the death penalty. The jurors imposed the death penalty again. Because of juror ignorance, bias, and dishonesty, Alexander—and Dr. Barrow—had lost.

He had put on a perfect case of mitigation. The jurors just could not grasp the scientific evidence; or they had refused, dishonestly, to do so. On appeal, the sentence was reversed again. Alexander had then withdrawn from the case because of a "conflict of interest" that he revealed to no one except the judge. He prayed that Stevens' new defense lawyer could save Stevens. He doubted it.

How he was going to wind up his practice and settle or try his remaining cases had become the issue. Besides Armstrong, there were just a few others. Next, Fernando Gomez, another murder case. This one had been continued for various reasons but was now ready for trial.

One of the tricks to being a good criminal defense lawyer was how you juggled cases. At one time, Alexander had two hundred. Now there were fewer and fewer. The Gomez trial would be brutal.

Chapter 21

May 9, 2005, Monday
Shelby County Criminal Court
Memphis, Tennessee
Fernando Gomez

It took almost a week to select the jury for the murder charges against Fernando Gomez, and then a week for the State to introduce its proof. They wanted to put every possible witness they could on the stand and make it a "mega-trial" if at all possible, thinking the best way to get the death penalty was by using angry witnesses by the dozen.

Alexander didn't bother to cross-examine many of the witnesses, with the exception of the question of time and the description of the killer. He wanted to get the exact time sequences of all the events, because he and his investigator on this case, Randy Fenton, had learned in his pretrial investigation some very important matters about time.

One of the key witnesses he interviewed was a World War II Coast Guard veteran, Samuel Thomas, who had been a security guard in an installation where he had become familiar with firearms and gunfire. He now lived in a rather large, mansion-type house in one of the more fashionable subdivisions in Memphis, Pleasant Valley.

Alexander and Fenton sat in the man's den in a pretrial interview session. Thomas said he remembered the time of the shooting as exactly seven o'clock, because he was watching a particular television program (which he named) when he heard the gunfire. He pointed to the rather large clock over the television set. "See that clock there? Well, Mr. Alexander," he said, "when I heard gunfire—I knew it was gunfire—I jumped up from my chair and ran to my kitchen. Let me show you."

He got up and made a quick sprint to his kitchen door, then stopped, turned, and stood in the doorway. "I walked right up to this door, but as I got to the door I turned and looked up at the big clock, and it was seven o'clock exactly."

He took a deep breath.

"I went outside and saw the shooting. I saw the gunfire, and I saw the man doing the shooting."

"Would you describe him to me please, sir?"

"Yes, sir. He had on a chocolate brown leather coat. I could see him clearly in the streetlight." He described in detail what he saw, including the man's face and long, blond hair.

Alexander paused and then said, "Mr. Thomas, are you sure of the time, the man's description, and the clothing?"

"Yes. I can't say who fired which shots, but the man I saw firing shots was wearing a chocolate leather coat."

"Could it have been navy blue?"

"No way."

"Could it have been, say, nylon navy blue?"

"No way."

"Well, thank you, sir. My investigator, Randy Fenton, is going to sit at your kitchen table and write down what you told us. If you don't mind, we'll move in there now."

The men entered the kitchen. Thomas sat down at the window side of the table, and Fenton sat next to him. Alexander remained standing by the doorway and explained what would happen.

"Mr. Thomas, when he's done writing everything down, he'll ask you to sign it. Since it might be a long time before a trial, you may eventually want to use this to refresh your memory, and we certainly need the statement. Do you mind?"

"No, sir!" Looking up at Alexander, he said, "Say, did you serve in the military?"

"Yes, as a matter of fact, I did."

"In which branch did you serve?"

"Marine Corps," replied Alexander.

"Oh, yeah? Well, I was in the Coast Guard, and it's always nice to meet another veteran."

"Yes, it is, sir, and I appreciate your cooperation very much. I've enjoyed meeting you."

Alexander reminded Randy to be sure to get a very accurate, detailed statement, and then he left. He knew he was onto something, and he now had his "reasonable doubt" theory to polish up.

Police officers had responded to a burglary-in-progress call in such a sloppy fashion that one of them had been killed. After knocking on the door and receiving no reply, one of the officers, gun in hand, had walked slowly to the rear of the large house. Out the back door came three men, running at full speed.

As the officer began to chase after them, he cried out, "Halt! Halt! Police Officer! Halt! Halt!"

The robbers did not stop. The officers who had gone into the house ran through the open back door, following the robbers into the backyard and out into the next street, which led to a nearby wooded area. One officer was shot and killed, but the chase continued into the woods. Two suspects were taken into custody.

This was a death penalty case. In the first stage of the trial, Alexander would argue that there was a reasonable doubt as to who fired the shots. During the course of the trial, he would pound away at each witness as to the time and to make sure no one could identify Gomez.

Gomez had testified he did not fire the shots but instead had picked up the pistol in the snow as they fled toward the woods after the shots had been fired. He testified that after the shooting, the gunman had thrown away the pistol. When Gomez came upon it lying there in the snow, he thought that he would need it for self-defense. He knew those police officers would come hunting and might just murder him, although he had not murdered anyone and had not wanted anyone to be hurt.

He testified he had been a former manager for a Federal Express office in San Diego and that he had come to Memphis with a friend he had met in Las Vegas. They were going to collect a gambling debt from a man named Canali, and he had come unarmed. The friend had brought another man with him, someone Gomez had never met and had felt a bit uneasy around. Until the police arrived, he thought the three of them were in the house for the purpose of collecting the gambling debt, which had sounded legitimate. But when the police knocked on the front door, his friend and the other man had fled out the back door, and he followed.

Alexander tried to develop his theory without much success, as the owner of the house, Vincent Canali, denied he was in debt to anyone, although he admitted he was a rather successful (millionaire) businessman and had been to Las Vegas many times and gambled and lost large sums of money. But he claimed those losses had always been promptly repaid, even one that had reached $250,000.

Years later, Alexander would encounter Mr. Canali in a Memphis bar, seated with a younger woman that Alexander recognized was not his wife at the time of the shooting.

"Mr. Alexander, won't you come over and join us?"

"Oh, thank you, Mr. Canali," he said, approaching the table. "How are you?"

Although the man gestured for him to sit down, Alexander remained standing.

"I'd like to introduce you to my new wife. You knew Hazel and I were divorced?"

"Yes, sir. I heard."

"Won't you sit down?"

"No, thank you. I'm in rather a hurry."

"Well," he said, "I'd like to tell you, sometime, what that shooting was all about."

"Oh?" Alexander was elated and caught completely by surprise. He had assumed he would never find out.

"Yes. Give me one of your cards, and I'll have lunch with you sometime and tell you what happened," Canali said with a smile. "You know, it was a tragedy that young police officer was killed."

"Yes," Alexander responded. "He was a friend of my wife's in college, and the case was a great mixture of emotions for all of us. I'm sure you and your family will never recover."

"I'm certain it's what brought about my divorce. It was so traumatic. My wife thought I had lied about the gambling debts. Anyway, I'll give you a call and tell you all about it someday, among other things."

Alexander nodded graciously.

"Good evening, Mrs. Canali, Mr. Canali."

Gomez had been convicted of first-degree murder, but the death penalty was avoided. He was sentenced to life in prison. He did not wear a chocolate leather coat. Upon arrest, it was navy blue and nylon. Alexander believed Gomez had indeed fired the shots and that Samuel Thomas was in error in his description. This error, he believed, had saved Gomez's life.

Mr. Canali never told Alexander "the real story."

Chapter 22

May 16, 2005, Monday
Department of Psychiatry at the University of Tennessee
Memphis, Tennessee
Ideas, once expressed

Earlier that day, Alexander had sat in his Memphis office, trying to concentrate on Armstrong's defense. He was not answering his phone. His attempts to contact Dr. Doug Booth had been unsuccessful, so he learned of no possible witnesses that way. The other experts he knew did not understand the adversary system. They would not testify for either side of a controversy. They wanted to be called by the judge, not a defense lawyer, as neutral witnesses. Except for one.

Alexander had received a reply from Dr. James Barrow, the molecular neurobiologist from El Paso whom he had hired in the Stevens case. He agreed to take the case. Alexander was excited. Dr. Barrow agreed with him that it was the amygdala, *and* they had an eyewitness.

There hadn't been an eyewitness in the Stevens case, and Stevens' confession did not cover the details enough to establish an instantaneous killing or the amygdala defense as defined. In his ignorance, Stevens failed to understand what Alexander had been trying to do. He had already been convicted, and Alexander's goal was for Stevens to serve life in prison rather than receive the death penalty. He had refused to cooperate.

In Major Armstrong's case, however, Armstrong could testify as to exactly what happened, and so could the bartender, the key to the case. All they had to do was try the case before she died. She had become very ill due to cancer.

Anyone could die. Defense lawyers had to remember that even those who weren't sick could just die. He would get prepared and push for an early trial date. Regardless, it would be months, and he had other cases to try that were on his schedule. This was his last year. He knew it. Everything had to go. He was ready to retire.

Suddenly, Alexander came out of what felt like a hypnotic trance. For a moment, he was frightened, wondering how long he had been "out," and then he realized he was late for a meeting of young psychiatrists where he was the guest speaker.

A few months before, he had been contacted by the head of the Department of Psychiatry at the University of Tennessee in Memphis and invited to speak to fifteen young psychiatrists who already had their medical degrees but had not completed their training in psychiatry. He remembered the conversation.

"Dr. Melborne, I appreciate your invitation to speak to these young men, but quite frankly, I think you may be wanting to present me to them more so they can decide whether I'm insane—or not—than to hear about my theory of crime and genetics."

"Oh, no, John, I'm sincere. I want you to talk to them about crime and genetics. You know, for a person without a scientific background or medical degree, you know more about this subject and have better ideas than anybody I know. Please come and be our guest. It's just a rather informal get-together at the home of one of these young men, and I think it would be a real good experience for them."

"All right. I'll accept."

As he approached the doctor's residence that evening, he wondered again if this was some kind of trap. He parked his car, got out, and walked up to the rather plain little house. He knew that this was how doctors lived until they got their medical degrees, and then they were almost always successful overnight and moved into large residences and accumulated large sums of money.

What a contrast to lawyers. He knew the public thought lawyers were rich, but he also knew most weren't. As a matter of fact, a lot of them had a hard time making a living. And he did know at least one doctor who had not been financially successful. He was sure there were probably others.

The door suddenly opened.

"John! Come on in," said Dr. Melbourne. "We're all here, ready and waiting with great anticipation."

He entered the room to greet fifteen smiling young faces and said to himself, *Boy, this is going to be fun!* Almost immediately he was asked to begin his talk. Someone handed him a cup of Irish coffee and a couple of doughnuts. He could drink coffee and eat doughnuts at any hour of the day or night.

He began by telling the doctors that someday medical students in their final exams would be asked to diagram the molecular structure of conditions such as the Oedipus complex. He asked if there was anyone in the room who would like to challenge that statement. Not one of the young doctors spoke.

There were only two women in the group. He spoke quite frankly, asking if it would be all right if he told a dirty joke before he made his presentation. Doctors, like lawyers, he thought, would like a dirty joke, notwithstanding the two young ladies. No one objected. He told the joke, and fortunately he got the laughter he wanted.

Now he began his formal presentation.

"It was not until the 1940s that we knew for certain that humans had forty-six chromosomes of DNA. DNA, as you know, is the logic of life. And yet it is still a mystery. The unraveling in 1953 of the DNA double helix was a great scientific event, like the splitting of the atom or Darwin's

Origin of the Species. It marked a turning point of a new science, molecular biology. We could at last explain and seek to understand life at the fundamental level—atoms and molecules.

"I'm going to briefly summarize a few facts about the human body. I know this will seem very basic to you doctors, but it is the basis of the criminal defense I've been asked to describe to you."

He smiled at the group. They seemed interested.

"A human consists of trillions of cells. Cells are chemical factories, each made of millions to trillions of tiny groups of atoms called molecules. About one third to one half of the cells are actually red blood cells carrying oxygen to the other cells, and each such cell is the record of billions of years of evolution, more historical than physical, performing a precision biochemical dance begun eons ago by its ancestors in the primordial ocean.

"The average cell contains millions of protein molecules, with four main types. Each cell is a society within itself. Inside the cell is a world about which Darwin, Freud, Dostoevsky, Shakespeare, the Biblical writers, and others before us could only speculate.

"The cell's nucleus, we now know, is dominated by bodies called chromosomes. Humans have 46, or 23 pairs. Some sources say that threaded end to end, the chromosomes of one cell would total more than six feet in length.

"Genes are a set of instructions within the DNA strings that determine what an organism is like: its appearance, how it survives, and how it behaves in its environment. Genes are always located at specific spots in specific chromosomes. As I've said, the logic of life revolves around the gene. DNA is the secret of all plant and animal life on earth.

"We're all genetically linked. According to studies at the University of California, Berkeley, and Emory University in

Atlanta, all humans today are descendants of one female who lived two hundred thousand years ago. I have with me the January 11, 1988, issue of *Newsweek* where their findings were reported, but I feel certain that all of you doctors are familiar with that scientific study. It is almost undisputed."

He held up the magazine cover, watching for reactions from his students, and then he continued.

"Another good resource is the book *Search for Eve: Have Scientists Found the Mother of Us All?* by Michael Harold Brown."

He was happy to see that several seemed to be writing down the name of the book.

"If all the DNA in a single human cell was placed end to end, it would be more than six feet long, but if all the DNA in *all* of the cells in a human body was placed end to end, it would reach the sun and back more than 50 times! I read somewhere that the DNA in a single cell contains instructions that would require in writing more than a thousand 600-page books, and a set of chromosomes contains as many different messages as expressed by the number 256 followed by 2.4 billion zeros. Of course, as scientific inquiry continues, numbers change, become more refined. The fact is, the numbers are huge. The particles are small. Does anyone disagree so far?"

Alexander wondered if he was boring or insulting these young doctors with this sort of talk. Well, they would not miss his enthusiasm. He smiled. The young doctors frowned. No one spoke.

"Now can anyone explain exactly how the brain and body function in making decisions, such as to commit a crime—murder, rape, burglary? Don't try to answer. No one can. I'll just keep asking why, and eventually you'll say you don't know. No one knows, I'm sure. And also, before you try to answer, remember we are not all created equal. Remember there are thousands of genetic, congenital defects that we know of—inherited at birth. Is *criminal personality* such a defect? Inherited? What if I could prove it? Scientifically, I mean."

"Mr. Alexander," a young doctor began, "may I quote Alexander Pope? 'Tis education forms the human mind; just as the twig is bent, the tree's inclined.'"

Alexander shot back. "What did Alexander Pope know about DNA? Harvard political scientist James Q. Wilson and Richard J. Hernstein, a Harvard behavioral scientist, argued several years ago in *Crime and Human Nature: The Definitive Study of the Causes of Crime*, one of the exciting books on the subject, that crime cannot be explained by social factors alone. There are now hundreds of books and articles that explore the genetic roots of crime.

"Ernest Hemingway, who among other accomplishments won a Pulitzer Prize in Fiction in 1953 with his novel *The Old Man and the Sea*, and then the Nobel Prize in Literature in 1954 for the same book, committed suicide with a rifle in Ketchum, Idaho, in 1961. His brother, Leicester Hemingway, also a writer, shot himself to death in 1981. Their father, Dr. Clarence Edmonds Hemingway, had fatally shot himself with a handgun in 1929. Each, it appears, was in a diabetic depression. What role did genetics play in these deaths? Does genetics cause crime in the same sense?

"Charles Dickens once said, 'The forces that affect our lives, the influences that mold and shape us, are often like whispers in a distant room, teasingly indistinct, apprehended only with difficulty.'"

"Mr. Alexander, what do you mean by 'defect'?" someone asked.

Alexander quoted from Lewis Carroll's *Through the Looking Glass,* using voice changes that he thought could only make it more interesting and memorable.

"'When I use a word,' Humpty Dumpty said, in a rather scornful tone, 'it means just what I choose it to mean—neither more nor less.' 'The question is,' said Alice, 'whether you can make words mean so many different things.' 'The question is,' said Humpty Dumpty, 'which is to be master—that's all.'"

Alexander smiled and glanced at his audience, hoping he had intrigued them, and then he asked if there were any questions. The students politely grilled him. It took about 30 minutes for the questions and answers.

"Okay. By your questions and comments, I take it that most of you disagree. That's okay. Most of you were trained in religion and psychology before you went to medical school, and you believed in free will before you got to medical school and before I started talking tonight. I had little chance of changing your mind—your opinion."

He shrugged.

"If you try to explain capitalism to a communist, you usually lose. If you try to explain to a cannibal why he should not eat human flesh, but to eat vegetables and other meats, you lose."

He was amused, but only one or two of the group seemed to share the humor. He went on.

"But what if I could scientifically prove my point? That there is no free will? Would you agree then?"

No one answered. Finally, someone said, "How?"

"Ah…." Alexander grinned. "Clone criminals!"

"What?" the same student replied. "Clone criminals?"

Alexander said again, "Clone criminals." Then he explained it to them.

When it was over, they looked anguished. Not one of them seemed to approve.

"Look," he said, smiling. "Most scientists today believe in some form of evolution and that changes in anatomy or behavior evolved 'for the good of the species.' All animal social behavior is subject to the same evolutionary forces as physical traits, as claimed by Darwin. Edward O. Wilson stated these ideas in his 1975 book, *Sociobiology: The New Synthesis*. In Wilson's words, 'The organism is only DNA's way of making more DNA. Beneath all the fancy courtship rituals, sexual reproduction is essentially a mechanism for transferring genes.'

"The organism, Wilson contends, does not live for itself. Its primary function is not even to produce other organisms. It reproduces genes, and it serves as their temporary carrier. Somehow, from within the organism, the gene communicates with other genes seeking perpetuation and dominance of their traits, at the expense of or with the cooperation of other genes."

"So what, Dr. Alexander?" said one of the women. "Assuming by cloning criminals that you can prove that humans do not have 'free will,' so what?"

"First, the title 'Doctor,'" said Alexander. "I'm not a doctor. I have a doctorate degree in jurisprudence, but lawyers are not called 'doctor.' It's because we are also arrogant—like doctors who like to be called 'doctor.'"

Almost everyone laughed.

"Secondly, let me quote the distinguished biochemist Edwin Chargaff, who said, 'If you can modify a cell, it's only a short trip to modifying a mouse, and if you can modify a mouse, it's only a step to modifying a higher animal, even man.' To define criminal personality or attack criminal behavior genetically is, I admit today, beyond our imagination. We don't even know a genetic theory to begin a quest to breed out crime by altering genes.

"To some of us, such ideas are no more than the black magic of Macbeth's three witches, stirring a cauldron of trouble. Others are perhaps horrified by the ghost of Adolph

Hitler, the political gangster, and the Third Reich—of evil human experiments almost beyond description and imagination. The Nazi holocaust should never be forgotten, nor Hitler's evil experiments in eugenics."

He paused to let that sink in.

"In 1982, an eleven-member presidential commission appointed by President Jimmy Carter submitted a report to the next president, Ronald Reagan. This report was called *Splicing Life: A Report on the Social and Ethical Issues of Genetic Engineering with Human Beings*."

He picked up a piece of paper he had brought with him.

"In the cover letters that went to the President, the Speaker of the House, and the President of the Senate, they wrote the following."

He read.

Some people have suggested that developing the capability to splice human genes opens a Pandora's box, releasing mischief and harm far greater than the benefits for biomedical science. The Commission has not found this to be the case. The laboratory risks in this field have received careful attention from the scientific community and governmental bodies. The therapeutic applications now being planned are analogous to other forms of novel therapy and can be judged by general ethical standards and procedures, informed by an awareness of the particular risks and benefits that accompany each attempt at gene splicing.

Other, still hypothetical uses of gene splicing in human beings hold the potential for great benefit, such as heretofore impossible forms of treatment, as well as raising fundamental new ethical concerns....

He looked at the group and sighed audibly.

"Some of the concerns that were expressed in this report regarding genetic manipulation had to do with the possibility of the creation of lab biohazards, theological and social considerations, the 'arrogance' of interfering with Nature, and the problem of crossing species lines and creating self-perpetuating 'mistakes.' Their concern even included the possibility of transplanting human genes into animals, to create subhuman hybrids as slaves. Listen to this—and remember, this was written in 1982."

He read from the paper again.

Could genetic engineering be used to develop a group of virtual slaves—partly human, partly lower animal—to do people's bidding? Paradoxically, the very characteristics that would make such creatures more valuable than any existing animals (that is, their heightened cognitive powers and sensibilities) would also make the moral propriety of their subservient role more problematic. Dispassionate appraisal of the long history of gratuitous destruction and suffering that humanity has visited upon the other inhabitants of the earth indicates that such concerns should not be dismissed as fanciful.

He set the paper down and paused, observing the looks on his students' faces.

"The commission found no evidence of using gene splicing for unacceptable political purposes, but they said that the role of eugenic theory in Nazi Germany's atrocities against Jews, slaves, and the mentally retarded made such fear valid. The commission also found no evidence of gene-splitting work that was of any fundamental danger to human values, social norms, or ethical principles.

"They did recommend, however, that the federal government establish a permanent and independent agency to oversee future genetic work. Such an agency would, of course, 'regulate' any human genetic engineering such as proposed in the cloning of criminals, and the agency might choose to outlaw such research until scientists know more about genetics. That was way back in 1982! Maybe we ought to clone good Christians first and see."

A few students quietly and hesitantly laughed.

"We may not be able to hang on forever to our Raggedy Ann dolls or our teddy bears. Society and the earth will change whether we like it or not. Human genetic experiments will be conducted. The questions are *what kind* of experiments will be conducted and *by whom?* Will the Russians or the Chinese be first? The Lenin, Stalin, or Mao of tomorrow may again reason that the 'ends justify the means,' as some have claimed the Italian philosopher Machiavelli's book *The Prince* promoted in 1532. There is no Anglo-church to stand in their way. The Roman Catholic Church has very little influence outside of the Western World.

"Western morality will not bar everyone on earth, even in this country, from experimenting genetically with humans. There are also perhaps billions of other planets with human life, like earth, over which we have no control or influence. It's estimated that over 95% of our Universe is uncharted."

He paused, ready to get to the point. He spoke more slowly now, with dramatic effect.

"Within the next two hundred years, genetic engineers may be able to alter the human body and create a crime-free society. We would then be able to drastically alter or abolish the Bill of Rights and other constitutional laws. Criminal defense lawyers, policemen, prosecutors, jurors, and judges would not be needed. There would also be no need for courts, jails, prisons, or the death penalty. We would treat criminals like anyone with a disease. Our treatment would be medical, not legal. There are many monumental philosophical, moral, and ethical dilemmas. Where do *you* stand?"

Students were looking around the room at their fellow classmates, none making eye contact with Alexander, some certainly hoping this was a rhetorical question. No one said a word. *They'll remember this lecture,* he thought to himself, and then he continued.

"In the time of Pythagoras, about 500 B.C., many thought the earth was flat. He proposed that it was round. A century and a half later, Aristotle declared it was a sphere. In the 1500s, Copernicus concluded it was round, and the sun, not the earth, was in the center of the universe.

"Around that same time, Bruno, the Italian monk, extended Copernicus's theories. He proposed that the stars were distant suns, that they were surrounded by their own planets, and that these planets might even be inhabited by their own kinds of life. Also, he was certain that we lived in an infinite universe with no center. Bruno has been called a martyr for science. They burned him at the stake!"

Now all eyes were on him.

"A hundred years later, Isaac Newton followed Bruno's lead and estimated the distance to nearby stars, on the assumption that their light was about the same as our sun. Many of Bruno's proposals and Newton's assumptions were finally scientifically established in the 1930s. Then Einstein came along and said Newton was wrong—and now there are scientists working out the kinks of Einstein's theories.

"It goes on and on. Creative thinking, discovery, announcement, backlash, acceptance, creative thinking, further discovery. On and on. Sometimes free thinkers are punished or sanctioned, but ideas, once expressed, take on a life of their own."

Alexander looked out at his audience of young medical students. He knew he had planted some seeds.

"Well, my hour is more than up. Thank you for having me as your speaker. I've enjoyed the challenge. I'll conclude with these remarks. Keep your minds open, always. The mind is like a parachute. It only works when open."

He smiled.

"Someday, doctors like you will be called upon to prescribe, for example, a therapy at the molecular level for, say, Hamlet. Could you do it? And suppose you were asked in court, as an expert witness, in the case of a murder by a man who had acquired an Oedipus complex in infancy, to identify this condition in its molecular form. You can't do it today, but someday doctors will. I so predict."

They clapped. He was glad the hour was over. It had been exhausting.

Chapter 23

May 17, 2005, Tuesday
Shelby County Jail
Memphis, Tennessee
George Edwards

She sat across from him at his large mahogany desk, motionless, crying softly. Armstrong's amygdala defense was again on a back burner. He had to focus his attention on another case. It was set for trial in a month.

"Mr. Alexander, I don't understand how they could accuse my husband of killing Mrs. Chapman. He didn't really *know* her. George is such a good man."

"Mrs. Edwards, I know you love him. He's your husband, but it is possible that he killed this woman. After all, as you admitted to me, he's been convicted of rape of a white girl before and was sentenced to fifteen years in federal prison. You met him at the prison in Texarkana. You knew his background."

"Mr. Alexander, George was a fine young man, a Christian. What happened to him years ago was because of a weakness. The Devil made him do it, and he's overcome that. He married me, and we were Christian folks. Went to church regularly, and he was just great to my children, all three of them, two of them girls—never did anything lewd or irregular, and was a *fine* husband. He worked every day. As a matter of fact, he is a plumber, and he met Mrs. Chapman only once, briefly, at Home Depot."

Alexander talked with her almost all afternoon. Her husband was in jail, and it was going to be a tough case. He had heard these facts before, but it was necessary to listen again. She insisted. He listened. He didn't like taking on clients who were in jail, because it was very difficult to visit them and work to investigate the case. Invariably, these were the ones who would sue you if the case was terminated in any manner they didn't deem successful. As a matter of fact, it had become rather common practice for the client to sue the lawyer whenever he lost. So the lawyer was forced to practice in a very defensive manner and almost had a conflict of interest from the beginning.

Alexander had to continually protect himself and to worry about "dotting every i" and "crossing every t," just as the medical profession had been doing for years, taking X-rays and doing procedures that really weren't necessary, just to prevent false claims and suits.

What a mess society was in. *We are the most litigious nation on earth, and it is getting worse, not better,* he often thought. The system had to be abolished if only for that reason and none other. There were just too many lawyers.

We didn't need lawyers, anyway. It would be nice if we had a lawyerless society—like China, he thought. No wonder the National Association of Criminal Defense Lawyers didn't want him to make any more speeches. They didn't want to hear that kind of talk.

As a matter of fact, most lawyers were enamored by the right to trial by jury, and jury trials, and really thought they were the champions of the accused and that everything was wonderful, whereas Alexander thought nothing could be further from the truth or even worse. Trial by jury, he knew, was a compromise, a battle of the wits, and it would be far better to settle disputes with a roll of the dice.

After Mrs. Edwards left, he sat at his desk for a while, considering the case, thinking, *Wouldn't it be nice if we could just roll the dice in the case of George, accused of this horrendous murder of one of the best-known schoolteachers in Memphis?* This was a tough one. She had taught German and art and was the most popular black teacher at Central High School in Memphis.

He remembered when Central was first integrated in 1957, and how things had changed. Today, here was a black woman who was highly respected, had distinguished herself, and now she had been murdered—at the hands of a black man. If white, black jurors would convict, and if black, white jurors would convict. Racial bias. No way to avoid it. This was a big problem.

Well, wait a minute, he thought. George hadn't been convicted yet. He was entitled to a presumption of innocence, certainly at least from his lawyer. *Maybe I should go down to the jail and ask George to go over his version of all this again before I reach my final conclusion.*

Alexander thought it was ironic that so many black *and* white men convicted of rape had the same appearance: young, slender, quiet, and nice. Of course, there were exceptions to any rule, and he was certain that there were some people who had been raped by big, husky, mean-looking football players, but he had just never represented any.

As a matter of fact, he hadn't represented many athletes. But he did recall representing the tight end of the Ole Miss Rebels, who had refused to put down a can of beer in front of the Hotel Peabody. He had thrown it down when he was told by the police to get rid of it and was arrested for a liquor offense. The judge in dismissing the case commented that Alexander should tell the coach that the State of Mississippi began in Memphis, at the steps of the Hotel Peabody! Alexander had been paid a rather substantial fee, so the dismissal was significant.

Alexander had also represented one other athlete—a wrestler. The case came on before Memphis Judge Nathaniel Grant, another Marine who, because of Marine comradeship, showed Alexander particular consideration and was always extremely polite. Though he was born a U.S. citizen, Judge Grant had a slight Italian accent, having been raised by

Italian parents. It especially came out when emotions roused His Honor. Of course, this rarely happened in court.

Alexander enjoyed Judge Grant's court, and on this occasion he had taken particular pleasure because of a bogus "prowling" charge against his client. After all, "prowling" was defined as moving around in a cat-like manner, something which this man certainly didn't do. As a large wrestler seen frequently on national television, it would have been quite comical had he been "prowling around" in a cat-like manner.

As a matter of fact, he didn't resist arrest, either. Instead, when the police officers confronted him on the front porch of his ex-wife's home at six in the morning, he tried to explain to them that he had been wrestling in Tulsa, Oklahoma, had arrived in town late at night, had a couple of beers, and decided to come over and make a child support payment.

They, of course, didn't believe all of that and tried to arrest him—but in trying to handcuff him, they were unable to get the handcuffs locked. The lateral muscles in his back were so well-developed, large, and bulging that it was impossible to bring the handcuffs together with the short chain between the two cuffs.

In court, Alexander demonstrated to Judge Grant and before a large courtroom audience this impossibility, and the charges were promptly dismissed. As he left the courtroom, he could see smiles in the audience. This was part of the pleasure of practicing criminal law: the discreet smiles or other signs of approval from the audience.

Now, George was locked up in the Shelby County Jail, accused of murder and rape. Alexander waited for him to be brought by jail personnel down to the jail interview room, and as he sat there, he reflected upon another case in Judge Grant's court. The charge had been "assignation," or making an appointment for sexual intercourse.

The statutory code section in Tennessee at that time provided for a misdemeanor if someone made such an appointment. As it turned out, his client was extremely attractive with a rather large, well-developed bosom, and she contended that she was employed by an escort service to model lingerie in the nude or to walk around in the nude, a service for which she was paid, sometimes by Visa or MasterCard. This was a professional service, and the company was listed in the Yellow Pages in Dallas, Atlanta, St. Louis, and other cities.

Nevertheless, the particular customer who had invited her to his room had kept trying to get her to engage in illegal conduct. She sensed this and kept avoiding making any illegal agreements, simply saying, "You'll get your money's worth."

The undercover police officer soon tired of this chicanery and flashed a large sum of money, a large roll of one hundred dollar bills, to which she had again responded, "I'm not promising you a blowjob, but you'll get your money's worth."

Whereupon, like the "big bad wolf" confronting Little Red Riding Hood, he shouted a signal to the other officers who had been in the adjacent room listening through the wall, and they entered and confronted her in the nude and arrested her. In trial, before Judge Grant, the testifying undercover police agent admitted that he had a Texas driver's license and had been pretending to be a legitimate customer, lying and deceiving her. (She couldn't lie to him!)

He admitted that the woman had said, as was revealed on a secret tape recording, "I'll not promise you a blowjob, but you'll get your money's worth," whereupon Alexander moved to dismiss the case, saying that there had never been any appointment for anything and that the officer didn't even know the definition of "blowjob"!

The courtroom roared. Judge Grant banged his gavel and insisted to Mr. Alexander that the officer, a vice undercover officer, certainly knew what a "blowjob" was.

"Your Honor, just let me ask him a question. You'll see. He doesn't know."

"He doesn't know what a blowjob is?" the judge responded in his Italian accent.

"No," said Alexander.

Judge Grant replied, "Ask him the question."

Alexander complied. "Officer White, state the technical definition of a blowjob."

Whereupon Officer White mumbled something vague about contact between the male penis and the female mouth, and Alexander shouted, "See there, Judge? See there? He doesn't know. He doesn't know!"

The courtroom roared, and the judge banged and banged and banged, finally dismissing the charges—reluctantly, of course.

This woman had a sister whose bosom was even more developed, and whose body was even more delectable. Alexander had represented her in a cocaine case, and the charges had also been successfully dismissed. She had moved to Ohio. Alexander mused to himself that these were the two best looking clients he'd ever represented.

He enjoyed thinking about those cases as he waited.

Bang went the door of the interview room, and in walked George Edwards, who seated himself at the jailhouse table. Alexander watched, a bit concerned. The expression on this man's face disturbed him. He leaned toward him and quietly spoke.

"Mr. Edwards, you seem quite irritated. What seems to be the problem?"

"Well, Mr. Alexander, how would you feel if you were locked up in jail under such circumstances?"

"What do you mean?"

"Well, I'm innocent of these charges, of course, and I'm being held without bond, and you know I have a thirteen-year federal sentence hanging over my head that I'm gonna have to go back and serve because of these charges."

"Mr. Edwards, if the charges are not true, they'll be dismissed, and you know that the federal parole authorities are not going to revoke your parole if they are dismissed."

"You want to bet? Are you going to guarantee that, Mr. Alexander?"

"No, I never guarantee anything, but I think you'll agree that's what ought to happen."

Edwards made no reply.

Alexander sighed and said, "But I'll be the first to admit that there's a big difference between the way things are and the way things ought to be. Let's discuss your case. Tell me again about these charges."

"I told you I was innocent."

"I understand, but tell me exactly what you know or remember about this case—what you've been accused of and what you know."

"Mr. Alexander, we have paid your fee in cash. There can be no continuance. I must get this over with by June. Do you understand?"

"Tell me about the case. Your wife fully supports you. You're lucky. She has told me a lot. I need your version."

George began to talk, slowly at first. He explained how he met or knew the woman, the teacher, but he was at home working on his car for over twelve hours the day she was abducted. He named all the people that could establish his alibi. His defense was alibi, or "I didn't do it."

Alexander was satisfied. He had indeed taken the cash, and he would be ready for trial by the end of this month. Major William Harrison Armstrong's amygdala defense would wait. He didn't even have a trial date set for the major.

Chapter 24

May 30, 2005, Monday
Shelby County Criminal Court
Memphis, Tennessee
Not a drop of evidence

Alexander couldn't think about the amygdala defense. It was time to defend George Edwards. He liked trying cases in Memphis. It was now his hometown, and he imagined people knew him and respected him. This gave him confidence. It also took less effort to represent the accused in Memphis. This was another murder case, and the defense was alibi. He had ten good defense witnesses!

He'd interviewed the pathologist who had performed the autopsy on the victim, the Central High School teacher. He knew, from the results of that examination and the candid nature of his conversation with the doctor, that he also had a chance to create at least one technical flaw in the trial. He wondered to himself what the real truth was, but he knew his client was not guilty. There was certainly reasonable doubt.

It was established by the first witness for the State that the dead woman was last seen entering the rear door of her house on November 26, 2004, and through another witness that there were screams heard shortly after she had been seen at her home.

Alexander thought to himself that this was great. They had pinned themselves down to an exact time and place, and he had an alibi defense. Ten witnesses. The best alibi defense he'd ever had. If his client had committed this crime, it certainly wasn't at the hour the State claimed.

The State called a pathologist to establish the cause of death. It was admitted by the pathologist on cross-examination that the cause of death was a crushed hyoid bone in the neck, which could have been just as easily caused by tripping or falling over a chair as it could have been from an intentional blow. Alexander was very pleased with his cross-examination, as he felt he had reversible error if the trial judge did not grant his motion for judgment of acquittal. The State closed its proof.

Alexander made his motion. "Your Honor, we move for a judgment of acquittal on the grounds that the State failed to prove a criminal cause of death, and in this failure of proof we are entitled to judgment of acquittal."

The prosecutor argued vehemently. The Court, Judge Felix Brown, was concerned but eventually overruled the motion. Alexander called his alibi witnesses. He had no intention of calling his client and letting the jury know about his prior federal felony conviction. Witness after witness established that George was at his home during the entire evening in question. It would have been impossible for him to have been at the scene of the abduction.

The woman's body had been found in a field more than a month after her death. Photographs were introduced showing her nude body. Even in that state, Alexander could see that she must have been beautiful. She'd been well loved, a great lady. What a tragedy.

The penalty was life imprisonment. What a crude and arbitrary way to decide such issues. There wasn't anything scientific about a trial. It was simply a battle of wits under archaic, ridiculous rules with all sorts of constitutional barriers. It was just plain arbitrary. A roll of the dice would be fairer.

Moreover, what if his client really was innocent and this jury found him guilty? It was frightening.

The key alibi witness was Edith Jones, a former television personality known by everyone in Memphis. She had retired and was very well thought of. He felt certain there were a number of jurors who would remember her.

"Mrs. Jones, did you call on the telephone the residence of Mr. Edwards on the night of November 26 at about six o'clock?"

"Yes."

"To whom did you speak?"

"Mr. Edwards."

"Would you tell us the gist of that conversation?"

She related the conversation and then commented, "I knew it was him because we talked about things that only he could know, and it was certainly his voice." She was sure it was two minutes after 6:00 p.m. She always kept notes.

The cross-examination by the State proved pointless, and the case went to the jury with Alexander feeling very good but knowing that there was a possibility of a guilty verdict. He felt certain the police had planted evidence, thinking in their own minds that Edwards was guilty and so that made it okay. It was this planted evidence—a cardboard drill box near the dead body, with the serial number traceable to the serial number of Edward's drill, which was found by the police in his pickup truck—that worried him.

He knew that jurors were totally unpredictable. Sure enough, the jury returned a verdict of guilty, but much to the shock and surprise of everyone in the courtroom, they charged him guilty of manslaughter, a lesser included offense. There would be no life in prison. Edwards would be sentenced by the judge a month later to the maximum term of ten years. Alexander considered this a great victory.

That evening as he drove home, Alexander turned on a local radio talk show. To his surprise they were discussing his case. The prosecutor had called. The other callers were upset listeners. These callers insisted that George Edwards was guilty of first-degree murder. *How can this happen?* they argued.

Finally, the jury foreman called. He insisted that the verdict was fair. The jurors had concluded the parties were on a date, and the woman had died by accident. There was not a drop of evidence to support this juror theory. Alexander wanted to call and object.

He knew better, though, and that call was never made.

Chapter 25

June 2, 2005, Thursday
Musings on the road
from Paris, TN, to Memphis, TN
The wrong expert witness

Paris is the county seat of Henry County, Tennessee, at the border of the State of Kentucky. Alexander had an ad in the area telephone book, but this was usually the furthest point of practice for him.

Years ago, Alexander had defended a young man in Paris, Tennessee, of unlawful possession of LSD. He had lost the case, but the Tennessee Supreme Court reversed the Tennessee Court of Criminal Appeals that had upheld the conviction because, as argued successfully by Alexander, the wrong expert witness had testified.

The lab expert who had actually identified the substance had been on vacation, and the prosecutor had called that expert's boss, the lab director, who testified to identify the substance as LSD, a controlled substance. The trial judge had overruled Alexander's objections that were based upon the constitutional right to confrontation, but the Tennessee Supreme Court reversed.

On retrial there were no errors, and the defendant was sentenced to seven years. He had been sentenced to only six years after the first trial, but the Tennessee Court of Criminal Appeals did not reverse this conviction. He served this longer sentence!

Several years later, in the same city, Alexander had represented a cocaine dealer who claimed to be Hank Williams Jr.'s drug supplier. Hank Jr., in fact, lived in Henry County across the street and down from the dealer, but the drug dealer was killed riding a motorcycle before trial.

The case was never tried. Actually, Alexander believed he was a liar and had learned how to avoid punishment by lying. It would have been his third conviction. Prisons educate criminals.

He was now driving to his last case in Henry County. He would be entering a guilty plea for methamphetamine manufacturing, reduced with a one-year sentence, and before trial the defendant could serve the sentence in a rehabilitation center in Shelbyville, Tennessee, day for day.

It was a sour victory. The search of the defendant's father's mobile home was probably illegal—no warrant, no consent—but he didn't live there. Technically, the illegal search could not be used, under the exclusionary rule to stop admission of the evidence: methamphetamine. The case was called, the plea entered, and Alexander said goodbye to the judge and prosecutor, both of whom he had known for 30 years or more.

He left and returned to Memphis via Highway 79. As he passed through Carroll County, traveling north to south, he thought about Confederate General Nathan Bedford Forrest and those cold days in 1862 when the Rebels crossed this area west to east. He had always wanted to find the old railroad bridge they had used to cross a Carroll County river, thus avoiding a federal trap at Huntingdon just before the battle at Parker's Crossroads.

Coming from Union City, General Forrest and his men had destroyed the bridges of the railroad near McKenzie. There was only one railroad coming through McKenzie at that time. After all that, they actually camped in McKenzie. After the war, the railroad would be extended from Nashville to Northwestern Kentucky, and on to St. Louis. It would be called the "Nashville, Chattanooga, and St. Louis Railroad."

Alexander just knew that General Forrest would have been a great lawyer. He had no formal education, but he was a natural warrior—and "mad as a pit bulldog" when in battle. He had character. Alexander was convinced he had done no injustice himself at Fort Pillow. He was also convinced the accusations arising out of his KKK membership were false.

As he traveled toward Jackson, to Interstate 40 and Memphis, Alexander thought about his hero Forrest and how false accusations can destroy lives.

Chapter 26

June 6, 2005, Monday
Office of John Alexander
Memphis, Tennessee
Bobby Jones

Natchez, Mississippi, is the oldest city on the Mississippi River, founded in 1716 by the French and named for the tribe of Natchez Indians who had resided there since the mid 1600s. Natchez was a perfect stop for the "Mississippi Queen" riverboat, as the town was born from riverboat trade. Today it is living testimony to the legendary days when river travel ruled the South.

It was also the hometown of Bobby Jones, whom Alexander would come to know as one of the strangest and most unusual clients he ever encountered. Before Alexander met him, Bobby had spent seventeen years in federal prison for bank robbery, including a five-year stretch for criminal contempt for failing to "snitch" on one of his federal cellmates—thanks to a Mississippi federal district judge who thought refusing to snitch was contemptuous and criminal.

Alexander first met Bobby in his office after he had been accused of a hotel burglary in Memphis, Tennessee.

Bobby entered his office, sat down, and without any sign of nervousness, quietly lit up a cigarette. Apparently he wasn't going to pay any attention to Alexander's No Smoking sign, and Alexander was not prepared to make an issue of it, although he was allergic to cigarette smoke.

"Mr. Jones, what is your occupation?"

"Burglar."

"No, I mean what do you do for a living?"

"Burglary." He laughed.

"I'm a professional burglar, although after serving seventeen years in federal prison for bank robbery, I quit and opened up a small grocery store in Mississippi. I was pretty good at creeping around at night without making noise. I became an expert in opening bank safe locks. After I got out of prison, I married, had a child, and opened a grocery store near Natchez, Mississippi.

"One day, an old buddy of mine from prison came along and wanted me to help him with one last burglary. I, of course, refused. After a lot of conversation, for some reason or another, I decided it was easier to go along with him than it was to argue him out of it.

"It did sound adventurous," he said, smiling. "This prison buddy was a motel/hotel burglar and expert at making keys that would fit the various rooms. It was his plan to go to Memphis to the River Inn, a pretty fancy place, and burglarize it. There was a big national golf tournament. We thought we could get a lot of cash, rings, that sort of thing. You know, golfers are notorious for carrying lots of valuable jewelry and money with them as they tour the country.

"After we got to Memphis, we checked into a room, and that night we set out to commit the burglaries. I made the mistake of going into the wrong room. I unlocked a door, and there was a woman and man naked in bed. I thought they were asleep, but apparently the woman was still awake.

"I took the man's billfold from the dresser. You know, it's crazy, but men always leave their billfold out where a good, sneaky burglar like myself can pick it up without any trouble. You go into the room. The billfold is lying out where you can pick it up. You pick it up, leave, and close the door. Go to the next room. Jewelry, cash, anything of real value, easily grabbed. You don't bang around making noise and taking chances." He laughed again.

"Anyway, as I started out the door, I saw the lady rise up in bed. I remember seeing her. Not bad looking tits. She

120

hollered, so I ran. I was wearing a suit of clothes for cover, so I would look like an ordinary guest in a hotel if anything did go wrong—as it had in this case. I got to the elevator and rode up, thinking everything was just great. A man and woman were on the elevator, and I rode up one more floor and got off and then walked back down to my second-floor room. I took off my suit of clothes and put it on the rack.

"It wasn't long before, much to my surprise, the police were knocking on my door. It was later that I found out what a stupid thing I'd done. The suit of clothes I carried was bright pink. You know, a Pepto-Bismol pink leisure suit. The lady had seen that pink suit! Must have glowed in the dark!"

He laughed again. "Of course, when they got to my room, they spotted it and arrested me."

Alexander shook his head in disbelief and said, "Jones, did you make any statements? You know, a confession?"

"Of course not, Mr. Alexander. You know I'm an experienced burglar, and I told the police I didn't wish to make a statement. I asked to see my lawyer. You know, the intelligent thing to do."

"So how did they know your room number?"

"Well, when all the commotion started, there was screaming and hollering and people running around the hotel. That man, he jumped out of bed and started down the hotel hallway chasing me, naked! But I guess he finally realized he didn't have any clothes on, and he turned around and went back. There was a lot of commotion for a while.

"My partner panicked, ran out of the hotel, jumped into his Cadillac, and took off down the street. And wouldn't you know, the cops answering the call passed the Cadillac and saw it was traveling at a high rate of speed. You know cops. They turned around and chased him down. Of course, he was experienced also, and he denied any implication in a burglary. He admitted he was staying at the hotel and what room he was in."

He shrugged his shoulders. "So, that's how they got to the room and the pink suit. Wasn't that crazy?"

Burglars always did interest me, Alexander thought to himself, and this one was certainly a puzzle. After getting a more detailed social history and discussing his client's military career and dishonorable discharge from the Navy, Alexander realized that this man had been a criminal almost from birth. First a juvenile delinquent, then a runaway, and then a whole lifetime of adult crime. A good portion of his life had been spent in prison. How could he make this mistake and risk going back to prison again? Unless, of course, as Alexander was prone to theorize, he was a genetic defect.

After making a fee arrangement and taking all the money Bobby could come up with, he wondered about the source of that money. Bobby said it was from the sale of his Mississippi store, since he knew he was going to need the money for attorney's fees and expenses.

Alexander pondered over the burglars he had known in his career. One in particular was a young man who had gotten his hand shot off after he had entered the backyard of another citizen for the purpose of burglary.

Now, this was no ordinary young man. He had admittedly burglarized more than six hundred residences without being caught. What was strange was he wanted to sue the man who had shot him for the loss of his hand, although he knew he was going to have to serve several years in prison.

Alexander had refused to represent him in such a civil suit. The young man's mode of operation was to burglarize houses, take just the valuable items, put them in a pillowcase, and bury them in the yards of the homes, under culverts, rocks, near trees or mailboxes, and then walk out of the neighborhood and return home by bus. Weeks later, he would return in a private automobile and pick up the loot.

This reminded him of another burglary by a young man who was caught, or rather chased down, by three prominent Memphis women after he had burglarized a house and was seen walking down the street with a pillowcase load of silverware and jewelry, whereupon three ladies—one, the mayor's wife; another, a doctor's wife; and the other, the wife of a car dealer—proceeded to chase him down the street. Although they never caught up with him, they did create enough trouble that eventually the police cornered the young man. He spent several years in prison. He, too, had a long career as a thief.

What drives men to burglary? Alexander wondered. *Why aren't there many female burglars? Or for that matter, lady "cat-like" bank robbers?* He had only known one female bank robber in his career, and what a dilly! She had walked into a bank in downtown Memphis and handed the teller a note demanding the sum of $680.23. According to bank policy, the teller gave her the money. The woman took the money, demanding the exact change, and left. Her husband turned her in for a reward under a Nazi-like program in Memphis known as Crime Stoppers, earning himself $1,000 plus a divorce! His wife spent ten years in prison.

Alexander remembered the case well, because after interviewing the woman in jail and taking her only possession, a worn-out automobile (which he gave to his investigator's girlfriend), he concluded she was suffering from PMS—premenstrual syndrome. He hired a psychiatrist to interview her, but she refused to be diagnosed as having PMS. She insisted she didn't suffer from any such thing and promptly fired Alexander. She later got a ten-year sentence by plea bargain, using a more expensive "tall building" law firm. He'd always wondered where she got the money to pay that firm. All he got was her worn-out automobile.

Well, burglars. Bank robbers. As he sat looking out his office window, this brought to mind another bank robber,

Philip Powell. Philip was a police officer. A very successful Memphis police officer. The trouble was his wife. She didn't like Memphis and wanted to move to Florida.

He quit the force, and they moved to Florida. In Florida, Philip got a job working in a private security office under a former Memphis police lieutenant who had also moved to Florida. Philip was living in the Hollywood, Florida, area when his wife announced that she didn't like the Cubans, the Spanish-speaking folks. She wanted to go back to Tennessee.

Philip quit his Florida job and took his wife and children back to Tennessee. He couldn't get his old Memphis police job back, so he drifted around doing odd jobs, waiting to see if he might get back on the Memphis police force. One day his wife told him if he came home that day without a good job, she was going to divorce him. She would leave the next day with the children.

That morning, depressed, Philip sat on the bank of the Mississippi River, thinking about his dilemma. He decided to pop a pill given to him sometime before by a friend at the Naked Lady Bar, who had said if he ever felt depressed to just take the pill. He would feel better. He took it. He really didn't know for sure what it was, but he had been told since then it was a Quaalude.

The next thing Philip knew, he was being arrested and charged with bank robbery. The police found $20,000 in the glove compartment of his pickup truck.

Philip had robbed the same First Tennessee bank as the woman with PMS, except his style was a little different. He went in with a briefcase, a dummy hand grenade, and a pistol. Of course, when Philip opened the briefcase and showed the grenade to the bank manager, she didn't know it was a dummy grenade. He told her she had just a matter of minutes to get the briefcase filled with money before he released the spoon on the grenade.

He had already pulled the pin. It looked real, like a small pineapple. He got the money. As he left the bank, unbeknownst to him, an automobile transmission repairman who was entering the bank saw him and became suspicious. He thought the mustache and beard Philip had on him were false, so he followed him.

Philip left the bank with cowboy hat, cowboy boots, and the false beard and mustache, seemingly undetected. When he sat down in his pickup truck and began to change his disguise, the transmission repairman saw him, knew something was wrong, and ran back into the bank just in time to encounter two officers who were entering the bank in response to a silent alarm.

A radio call went out for an old white and yellow Ford pickup truck. The truck was spotted at a downtown Memphis gas station by two officers, one of whom was female. She explained to her partner that this couldn't be the truck, because the driver was Philip Powell, who used to be her police partner! He couldn't be the bank robber!

As a helicopter hovered overhead and the two officers walked up to confront Philip, he blurted out, "What's all the commotion? Why the helicopter? I haven't robbed any bank!"

At trial, with the defense of insanity—and expert testimony—Alexander was able to persuade the jury to come back with a conviction of the lesser included offense of robbery and a sentence of ten years. They had beat the charge of bank robbery, which in Tennessee carried a sentence of 40 years. Alexander was told later that one of the jurors wanted to give Philip 40 years. The others refused to give him more than ten, one of the jurors saying, "Why, he was a former policeman!"

Strange as it may seem, Philip told Alexander after the trial that if caught, he had actually expected to be prosecuted in the federal system, where the penalties were much less.

Chapter 27

Jury selection began for the burglary trial of Bobby Jones. The first witness was the hotel victim whose billfold had been stolen, the one who had run down the hallway in the nude. He was an arrogant man from Connecticut.

Alexander was lying in wait for cross-examination, but he was having difficulty focusing on this case. He kept thinking about Major Armstrong and the amygdala defense. He was going to get a trial date as soon as this case was over.

"Good morning, sir. My name is John Alexander. I'd like to ask you a few questions. Now, you've just testified on behalf of the prosecution that your billfold was taken, and you've identified my client, Bobby Jones, as the man who took your billfold. Is that correct?"

"Yes."

"Well, now, you were in the hotel room. By yourself or with someone else?"

"By myself."

"Oh. You're certain there was no one else in the bed?"

No answer.

"Sir, isn't it a fact you were in the bed with a naked female, who was the one who actually saw the person taking the billfold? You never saw the person until she shouted."

"That's not true."

"As a matter of fact," Alexander continued, "you never saw the thief clearly enough to identify him or her, did you?"

"That's not true. It was your client. I remember correctly. I saw him creeping out of the room."

126

"Was the room dark?"

"Yes."

"Were the curtains drawn?"

"Yes."

"Were they those heavy hotel-type curtains to keep out the light?"

"Yes."

"Wasn't this an expensive hotel? The River Inn in Memphis? It is one of the nicer hotels, correct?"

"Yes."

"Were there any lights on in the room?"

"No."

"Were there any hall lights on?"

"No."

"Then how could you see this person? It was 3:00 a.m."

"Look, I saw him. That's him."

"Let me ask you this question. Do you have a wife back in Connecticut? A woman other than the woman in the room? And I want to remind you I have a recorded statement taken from you five days after the alleged crime. You remember talking to me on the telephone, don't you?"

"Yes." He looked a little shaken. "What do you mean recorded? You didn't record our conversation, did you?"

"Yes. And didn't you admit to me then that you were in bed with another woman?"

"Um, no...I never made such a statement."

"Would you like me to play the recording back at this time? That may jog your memory."

"No. I could have said that. I'm not sure. I could have."

"And didn't you admit to me during that conversation that she was the first one to scream?"

"I don't remember."

Alexander continued his scorching cross-examination, knowing at least he had a chance with the jury.

But when they returned a verdict of "guilty" for his client, Bobby Jones, he was very depressed.

If the judge's ruling a month later at sentencing hadn't granted his client probation, he would have been even more depressed. The trial judge had apparently concluded the witness/victim lied. It was His Honor's way of doing justice. Maybe he just liked Bobby, as Alexander did.

It wasn't long after that trial that Alexander received a telephone call about Bobby from an assistant United States attorney in Washington, D.C., who wanted to get Bobby's cooperation with respect to an arson case in Hattiesburg, Mississippi. He wanted Bobby to identify a prominent former Mississippi district attorney as an arsonist, saying Bobby knew the facts and was a personal friend of the torch man.

Alexander said he would call Bobby. Bobby said he would cooperate, because he had ended his life of crime and wanted to clean up as much as he could. He had never been a snitch, and he had spent five years in prison for refusing to be a snitch, but times had changed.

That next Monday, they were to appear before a grand jury in Jackson, Mississippi, and were to fly down together. When Alexander received a late-night telephone call at about 2:00 a.m. on the Saturday before that Monday, he was shocked to learn Bobby's wife had been found murdered on their sofa, a large overdose of heroin having been injected into her left arm.

"Mr. Alexander, my wife did not use or abuse drugs. She was murdered, and you know why. They want to keep me quiet, so they've killed her. Now what do I do?" Bobby asked, terribly distraught.

"You'll have to make that decision, Bobby. I'll go if you want to."

"I've made the decision," he replied. "We'll go, and after I testify before the grand jury, I want to relocate, change my identity, and my son's, and start over. Can you help me?"

"Sure. I'll get the judge's permission for you to move just about anywhere."

"Thanks."

Afterwards, Alexander would not hear from Bobby again until ten years later, when he received a card saying that all was well and he had just gotten back from a school Halloween party where he had been one of the chaperones for the children.

Alexander recalled that when Bobby got probation, one of the letters presented to the judge was a letter from the first-grade teacher of Bobby's then six-year old son. The teacher had stated she was very impressed with Bobby, because he always came to all school functions, and she remembered him best for bringing the children candy at another Halloween party. "What a model person he was at the party for these first graders," she had said.

Chapter 28

June 22, 2005, Wednesday
Office of John Alexander
Memphis, Tennessee
Another delay

Alexander finally had a date for Willie Armstrong's case. It would be first on His Honor's calendar. Alexander now needed to muster the character witnesses. Dr. Barrow was ready. He was coming to Memphis to interview Willie Armstrong in the Memphis jail.

When it was time to interview the character witnesses, Alexander would speak with Army Airborne Ranger Curtis Newhouse, from Corinth, Mississippi. Curtis had been stationed in Central America with Armstrong and had said over the phone that he knew him well. He was a retired sergeant major, and he insisted he would come at his own expense. Major Armstrong was his hero, he said. He had saved everybody's life in an ambush, including several Army Airborne Rangers, two recon Marines, and a Navy SEAL. Armstrong's character and courage were beyond question.

"Incidentally, Mr. Alexander, I'm white," he had concluded, "if you can't tell from my southern voice."

That afternoon, Alexander received a telephone call from the Clerk's office. Armstrong's trial had been continued. The trial judge had been seriously injured in an auto accident. He was in a Memphis hospital, alive, recovering.

Alexander was devastated. He knew Armstrong, in jail, would be more than disappointed. He would try to get the bail set and reduced. Under these new circumstances, he thought he would have a chance, but bail was denied. The trial date was again stalled.

Chapter 29

July 11, 2005, Monday
Office of John Alexander
Memphis, Tennessee
The KKK

The buzzer on the intercom was loudly vibrating. It was a new case. "KKK members," Ann said. This piqued Alexander's attention. His work for Harry Prince, the man who had been accused of illegally importing marijuana, was finished, and he didn't need any new cases, but he would talk to them out of curiosity. He was retiring, but....

After a few minutes of conversation, Alexander told the "KKK men" to come to his office that afternoon at 1:00. "Don't be late," he said. "I'm busy."

At 1:00, the KKK men arrived, on time. Their names were John Simmons and Vernon Jones.

Alexander wanted to make one thing clear. "I need to ask you guys some more questions. I'm afraid of a conflict of interest. Do you understand my point? Conflict of interest?" He waited for their response.

"What's that?" asked Jones with a puzzled look. "Conflict of what?"

Alexander ignored the question. What bothered Alexander was how Simmons kept getting up from his chair and going over to his seventeenth-floor office window and spitting out of it.

Finally, irritated, Alexander asked, "Why are you spitting out of my window?"

Simmons quickly turned his head and said, "Come see for yourself. There's a nigger down there, and I'm trying to hit him."

"You're trying to spit on his black head from a window seventeen floors up?"

"Sure. He's black."

"Sit down."

"Sure."

"Now, look. Obviously, since you guys are members of the Ku Klux Klan, you'd want to know what I feel about the Klan before you discuss this any further with me or employ me. Right?"

Both men nodded affirmatively.

"Well, I'm not a member of the Klan, I don't support the Klan, and don't like the Klan. But I've represented murderers, rapists, burglars, drug traffickers, perverts, child molesters, and all sorts of accused people involved in things I didn't like. So, you see, I *can* represent you. There's no real conflict of interest. I need a fee arrangement, a retainer."

Both men stared at him for a moment, and then Simmons spoke again. "You mean money?"

"Right."

"How much?"

"Five thousand."

"Cash?"

"Right. Cash. In advance."

"We can get it. The Grand Wizard will bring it. He'll be here tomorrow from Birmingham, Alabama. Can you meet with him?"

"Sure. Just have him call my office in the morning, and I'll squeeze him in. I don't have any trials or court appearances tomorrow."

Chapter 30

July 12, 2005, Tuesday morning
A restaurant on Union Avenue
Memphis, Tennessee
Nothing but a parasite

At about 10:00 a.m. the next morning, the phone rang. Ann said the Grand Wizard wanted to meet him at a local restaurant, Shoney's on Union, to which Alexander agreed. Though he felt this was quite suspicious, he got in his car and started on his way.

As he drove along, he recalled the sordid history of the KKK, which had been created in Pulaski, Tennessee, and whose first imperial wizard was one of Alexander's great heroes, Nathan Bedford Forrest, the Civil War general. Alexander had never liked the Klan. As a matter of fact, in earlier days, he and his wife had participated in a rally in Franklin, Tennessee, where they had publicly protested the Klan.

He remembered his wife standing there holding a sign.

THE KLAN IS NOTHING BUT A PARASITE
THAT INFECTS OUR SOULS

He couldn't really remember the rest of the words. She was so strongly against the Klan, he wondered how she would feel if he made this fee arrangement and it became public. Anyway, he would have to tell her. Was this a conflict of interest?

It was believed that the Klan had been founded as a social club on Christmas Eve, 1885. Six Confederate soldiers, bored during a Christmas Eve meeting, sat around the fireplace in the law office of Judge Thomas M. Jones and came up with the idea of the club. As Alexander recalled, according to one historian, one of the six suggested the name "The Merry Six." Another, who had studied Latin and Greek, suggested the Greek "kuklos," meaning band or circle.

From that evolved the name "Ku Klux Klan," or "Knights of the Ku Klux Klan." The Klan adopted regalia and robes, and chose a spooky abandoned house on the western outskirts of Pulaski as its regular meeting place. Klansmen in white robes and pointed hats began trying to frighten blacks by pretending to be ghosts of the Confederate dead—all of which did frighten superstitious blacks.

Two years after its founding, in 1867, Confederate General Forrest became the Klan's first imperial wizard. Throughout 1868, he went on a campaign creating new chapters and advising.

Old Confederates had lost their wealth and in many cases their health and homes, as well. They had lost their right to vote, lost their slaves and their slave labor. The Klan became an instrument to offset the Loyal Leagues, black organizations which some whites called the Nigger Klan in those days. The KKK became an instrument to "move the bottom rail back to the top." After all, the true "bottom rail" was, as a result of Civil War, now on top!

Some historians say that Forrest wanted to combat unfair, retaliatory practices associated with Reconstruction. Whether or not that is true, in 1869, due to what he deemed was its having become "injurious instead of subservient to the public peace," he attempted to disband the KKK and got out.

The Klan fed on hatred, fear, and ignorance—no matter how "noble" some thought its beginning. It became an organization of idiots, an "Invisible Empire." Its modern activities are questioned by the FBI, ATF, and other law enforcement authorities as criminal.

But Forrest had been the Civil War's greatest soldier, and Alexander loved him for that. Sherman had said, "That Devil Forrest must be hunted down and killed, if it costs ten thousand lives and bankrupts the federal treasury." Forrest had enlisted as a private. He entered the army worth a million and a half dollars. He came out a beggar—and a lieutenant general.

Alexander's favorite story of Forrest was his encounter with Colonel Robert Green Ingersoll, whom Forrest captured near Lexington, Tennessee, on December 18, 1862. The two cavalry officers met as the Yankee soldiers were fleeing. According to the story, Forrest arrived on horseback and saw Ingersoll. He pointed to the fleeing cavalry men and asked, "Who's in command of these troops?"

Ingersoll replied, "I don't know."

"Who *was* in command?" amended the General.

"If you'll keep the secret," said Ingersoll, "I'll tell you. I was."

Colonel Ingersoll was paroled and returned to Illinois to become a great orator, politician, and lawyer who popularized a higher criticism of the Bible, a humanistic philosophy, and a scientific nationalism which qualified him as the "bulldog" for Charles Darwin in the United States. He died in 1899 in New York. Forrest and Ingersoll became great friends, and until his own death in 1877, Forrest never lost an opportunity to visit Ingersoll.

Arriving at the restaurant, Alexander saw his clients sitting at a table with an older man. He entered and introduced himself.

"I understand you're one of the best ten criminal defense lawyers in Memphis," the Wizard began.

"That's right," replied Alexander, always selling himself.

"Where did you go to school?"

"Vanderbilt Law School, Nashville, Tennessee, and my undergraduate years were at the University of Washington in Seattle. Do you know the schools?"

"Vanderbilt's a good school. We have a lot of Klan members in Davidson County. Don't know anything about Seattle, though."

There was a long silence as the Wizard sat there almost motionless. Alexander began to grow impatient.

"What did you want to talk about?" he inquired.

"Your fee, but before we talk money, Mr. Alexander, are you a member of the Klan?"

"You already know I'm not. Or if you don't, you ought to." Alexander repeated the conflict of interest speech he had made to the KKK clients the day before.

The Wizard didn't like this.

Alexander continued. "Look, I'm deeply committed to the right of any person to zealous and effective assistance of counsel, no matter how unpopular and no matter how heinous the alleged offense. This is the foundation of our democratic system of justice and is a matter of constitutional right. Representation does not constitute an endorsement of a client's political, economic, social, or moral views— or activities."

The Wizard looked as if he had just eaten something distasteful. "Mr. Alexander, I want you to read a book, or parts of a book."

"What's the title?"

"The Bible."

"You want me to read the Bible?" He almost laughed.

"Yes," said the Wizard. "Do you know why?"

Alexander knew the Klan claimed biblical support for its views.

"No," he replied. "I won't read the passages you want me to read, which I'm sure I've already read, unless you agree to read *my* book."

"What do you mean, *your* book?"

"I've got a book I want you to read."

"What's it about?"

"It's about the evolution of human intelligence. *The Dragons of Eden,* written by Carl Sagan. Have you ever heard of it?"

"I'm not reading any book about evolution."

"And I'm not reading any passages from the Bible." He sighed, shaking his head. "Look. You can't hire a better defense lawyer. There's not a better gun for hire in this town. I'm your man. Did you ever see the movie, *Shane*?"

"Yes."

"Then you know what a hired gun is. You want the best. That's me. Your men are in trouble. You know what I mean?"

The Wizard handed Alexander the money in an envelope under the table. He said Alexander could count it. Alexander told him it wouldn't be necessary, and that he trusted the Wizard's mathematical ability. They departed with Alexander telling Simmons and Jones to show up at his office at 2:00 p.m. that afternoon.

Chapter 31

July 12, 2005, Tuesday afternoon
The office of John Alexander
Memphis, Tennessee
The most ignorant men

At about two o'clock, Alexander and his two KKK clients (he couldn't help thinking of them as that) resumed their conversation in Alexander's office.

Alexander began. "Okay, what's this all about?"

Simmons replied. "Well, me and Vern were—"

"You mean Vernon?" Alexander was feeling annoyed.

Vernon inched his chair closer to Alexander's desk, his eyes almost closed, barely visible. He never spoke a word.

"Yeah. Vern," Simmons continued. "We were told to take care of this guy who was an informant. He worked for the ATF. Alcohol, tobacco, and firearms."

"You mean a *federal* government agent?"

"Yeah."

"You mean he had infiltrated your organization?"

"Yeah, and it was our duty, voted according to Klan rules, to punish him for his anti-Klan activities. So we got some yellow paint—you know, the kind they use to put the stripes in the highway—and a bed pillow that was already no good. I mean, Vern didn't even want it. We dumped him out naked on Poplar in East Memphis near Interstate 240. Just like the TV and papers said. You know, took his clothes off, threw the paint on him, threw the feathers. Fixed him up good, didn't we?" He looked at Vern and laughed.

"Yeah," Alexander said, "and got yourself criminal charges, including kidnapping."

"Well, look, Mr. Alexander," said Simmons nastily. "You're the best. You've been paid. Now get us out of this."

After they left, Alexander sat there in his office staring at his license to practice law, his license from the Supreme Court of the United States, and his university diplomas and honorable discharge from the Marine Corps, thinking, *How absurd.* Here he was representing the kind of individuals he absolutely despised.

And yet, deep down inside of him, he admitted to himself, he didn't really like most black people, either. He was totally baffled by his feelings and had never understood why. *Maybe all this is genetic*, he thought. *Really genetic*, he thought. *Maybe personality is a product of birth. Environment or life experiences don't really have much to do with it.*

Who were the people who joined Klan organizations? These were two of the most ignorant men he'd ever met. They were so stupid, so ignorant, it was almost incomprehensible.

He reflected. Every Klan member he had ever met or come in contact with or read about was also stupid. Ignorant. How could so many white people with such a low level of intelligence band together with such a ferocious hatred for black people—not to mention all the other terrible things they stood for?

He thought about his own stupid racist feelings. How was he going to convince a judge of their innocence? He had already decided there was no way he could get a jury in Memphis without a substantial number of blacks being in the jury pool, and some would become jurors in the case. He was convinced these blacks would be incapable of being fair to these white men. He didn't even have a defense, let alone "the best" defense, to use the words of one of his favorite lawyers, Professor Alan Dershowitz of Harvard.

He remembered Dershowitz's rules and his criticism of the criminal justice system. Dershowitz was another lawyer like himself and Seymour Wishman, author of *Confessions of a Criminal Lawyer*, who were sick of the horrors of the system. There were lots of lawyers like his good friend

Wayne Payne, a criminal defense lawyer, who had come to see through the system and realize that it was basically flawed and could never do the job envisioned by men.

Alexander continued to reflect. He felt terrible.

Those old architects of criminal justice were God-fearing white men who, when they created the system we adopted from England, had based it upon the concept of "free will," which as Wayne and Alexander had discussed many times was the actual basis for criminal responsibility. After all, those architects were extremely religious. They really believed God the Creator existed and that there was a judgment day, and the Lord would punish those who had sinned. Society had created a mini system on earth with all sorts of religious assumptions.

But they left out the New Testament's basic doctrine, "forgiveness." Oh, they would say, "Not true. There are all sorts of examples of forgiveness, such as parole and probation and community sentencing." But Wayne and other lawyers, including himself, knew criminal justice was doomed. Here he was with another classic case of a couple of genetic defects!

If we could just alter their genes. You know, take them to a hospital instead of a court and do something good. Treat them like we treat the mentally ill or the mentally disabled. But, of course, society wants them punished. This is our system. The culprits chose evil! Punish them!

He continued his train of thought. According to the dominant religion, there would be a judgment day. No one escaped the wrath of God. All criminals would be caught and punished. So why punish anyone? God would do it. It was absolutely necessary that everyone understood. Wouldn't this deter them? A "lake of fire." Eternal death!

He went over in his mind again the reasons or labels for why criminals were punished, remembering the words of one of his old law professors long since dead, that literature and expert opinion studies had confirmed the only reason to punish anyone that had any possible validity was "just desserts." But revenge just didn't seem to be a good enough reason. Keeping in mind the Bible, he thought of a verse. "Vengeance is mine...saith the Lord." Vengeance just didn't seem like enough of a reason.

He knew the criminal judge for those two Klansmen, a good Catholic, would not listen to any of Alexander's babble, and besides, you couldn't educate judges. They were either educated or uneducated, and most of those he had met were uneducated. Oh, they had formal educations, degrees, and had attended universities, but most were still just ignorant. They didn't think critically. The reason you made speeches to judges and jurors was to satisfy your client who was paying the bill. To make him *think* he had a fair trial.

Some jurors were easier to mold than others—and once in a while, jury arguments were effective. But he wasn't going to take a chance on a jury with these Klansmen. These defendants were just too ignorant. They were Klansmen and couldn't testify. Besides, what would they say? It would be, he thought, another thousand years or more before race didn't play an important part of any Anglo-American trial.

He kept thinking. Life was just a series of compromises. We take great pride in thinking of ourselves as a people who do not compromise beliefs or virtues. The truth is, we do.

The Constitution itself was a compromise. Compromise was a virtue. Were lawyers just gladiators whose purpose was to win? To do what the client wants? What about the interest of the public? Were lawyers really just hired guns? Is a lawsuit like chivalric combat, involving intense competition, a public arena, structured rules of conduct, and reciprocal courtesies? Do the laws of the tournament apply?

Alexander continued this train of thought. Never strike with the edge or the point—only the flat end of the sword. Never strike the back, or fight out of rank, or wound the horse of an adversary. Fair play? Don't press an advantage on outnumbered foe or against a worthy opponent who has suffered a mischance.

He thought of Lancelot and the book *Le Morte D'Arthur.* What would Sir Lancelot do as a modern lawyer representing a KKK member? Or Ivanhoe? Do we give the State a second chance if a mistake is made? What was "zealous" representation?

To hell with the rules of chivalry, Alexander thought.

Yes, he would be the champion of his clients. Courage, fidelity, dignity, resourcefulness, strength, and composure— even when the cause was doomed. He was an advocate, first, above all.

A little over two weeks later, standing before the judge, having worked out with the prosecutor a plea bargain of two years imprisonment each, he begged for probation and got it, much to his amazement and the joy of his clients who by now he despised even more.

He didn't like government snitches, or informants, or (as called by some in modern criminal jurisprudence) "cooperating individuals," any more than anyone else did. This had been a "snitch" of the ATF, a federal agency that did not enjoy a good reputation with criminal defense lawyers because of its use of snitches or spies, eavesdropping, and secret tape recordings.

All law enforcement agencies were guilty of such conduct, but the *federal* government agencies had mastered such tricks, even beyond those of the Nazi government. He thought the morality of the administration of criminal justice should be higher than the morality of warfare between nations.

And it wasn't.

Chapter 32

August 8, 2005, Monday
On the way home
Memphis, Tennessee
Who sent the signal?

Alexander met with Dr. Barrow at his office, and then Dr. Barrow interviewed Willie Armstrong at the jail. Barrow was satisfied. He could support the amygdala defense and do the neuroanatomy, neurobiology, the works. He would use 3' x 5' posters and be responsible for all the technical drawings: brain, neurons, neurotransmitters, and so on. He would explain fully the limbic system, the amygdala, and the hippocampus.

Dr. Barrow needed to know, however, *why* the word "nigger" had been the trigger. He was puzzled. He knew the memories colored by the amygdala were subconscious, and he could explain such to the jury, but why had such a word provoked such violence at that moment in time? Was there anything else?

Alexander intended to interview the grandmother again, as well as five or six Marine buddies for an answer. Starting on Tuesday, he would be bringing in witnesses. *Hope they all show up,* he thought to himself. For now, he would do some work on other files and go home early. He couldn't wait to answer this question for Dr. Barrow.

On the way home, Alexander inserted into his CD player the doctor's recording of his interview with Willie Armstrong. He wanted to hear what Dr. Barrow had said to Willie. The recording began to play. He listened carefully to the doctor's questions and Armstrong's answers.

He skipped along until he came to the end of the interview and found a question Willie had asked, "Dr. Barrow, can you explain to me my amygdala defense? Start with the basics."

"Yes, certainly," Dr. Barrow replied. "If you are standing still and decide to take a step, the movement in your leg involves axons that originate in the movement control region in the frontal cortex of the brain, just behind your forehead. These axons travel uninterrupted to the base of the spinal column in your lower back. If you decide to kill someone consciously, and you move your hand with a knife in it, axons carry a signal to muscles to contract, move, contract, move."

Alexander could barely hear Willie's voice—a word, or a grunt.

"At the end of each axon is a terminal that communicates with a receiving neuron, muscle, or gland. Terminals most often form connections with things called dendrites, but they also contact cell bodies or other axons. The long axons from the cells in the frontal cortex cause your leg or arm to move—that is, contract. The axons of the receiving cells extend out and terminate at muscles in the leg or arm.

"The arrival of signals at the muscle leads to contraction and thus movement. Most neurons have only one axon. However, each axon branches out many times before it ends. The dendrites can bring in one to 100,000 signals, and the axon sends out only one signal or the same signal to many terminals. At the terminal is a tiny space, billionths of a meter, and the electrical impulse, called an 'action potential,' crosses the gap via a chemical called a neurotransmitter secreted into the gap by the neurons.

"Signals from the sensory receptors in the eyes, ears, nose, and fingers are sent to the frontal lobes—the cerebral cortex. This information, these signals, are transmitted to the dendrites by neurotransmitters. Got it?"

There was a pause on the recording. Alexander didn't hear Willie's voice. After a few seconds, the doctor resumed.

"These gaps or synapses are the key to self and decision-making. But who sent the signal? The frontal lobes? You? Or, perhaps the amygdala—unconsciously? And not involving the frontal lobes or cerebral cortex. That is, *not* you. Got it?"

Silence.

"You can calculate current, voltage, and resistance in axons, but the issue in your case is *who* sent the electrical signal? What part of your brain and why? It's an electrochemical event. The balance between excitatory and inhibitory inputs determines if a neuron will fire."

The doctor was warming up. His voice was sounding more and more animated.

"Glutamate is an excitatory neurotransmitter. The amino acid GABA is an inhibitor. GABA regulates the flow of traffic. They are together responsible for much of the neurotransmission of the brain. They work by attaching to molecules called receptors on other cells.

"Each cell is completely enclosed by a membrane. This membrane covers the axons, dendrites, and entire body of each cell—even if the axon is several feet long! The resting potential of the cells is minus 60 mV, or 60 one-thousandths of a volt. 60 millivolts more negative than outside the cell. When excited by the input of other neurons, it becomes more positive—"

Finally, Willie spoke.

"Dr. Barrow, let me interrupt you. I'm lost. And I'm very tired. You've lost me. I trust you. I'll go along with the defense. I had no idea it would be this complicated."

Dr. Barrow replied, "Thanks. It's okay. Just trust us."

Alexander clicked the tape off. He began to think about how the doctor had described the amygdala defense. It was very technical. Most citizens, most jurors, knew nothing about science, let alone neurobiology or neuroanatomy. Out of 100 potential jurors, only six or seven would be scientifically literate!

Besides bias and dishonesty, ignorance in 2005 was an almost insurmountable barrier to justice. *Voir dire* would be paramount. Potential jurors would have to be questioned to determine if they were suitable. He would have to use juror questionnaires and hire a real expert consultant to help. He must somehow weed out those most ignorant, biased, and/ or dishonest. It was an almost impossible task. He thought about Don Quixote.

The telephone rang.

"Mr. Alexander, my name is Murphy. Donald Murphy. I'm from New Madrid, Missouri. I understand you represent Major Armstrong. I served with him during the Persian Gulf War. The first one. I understand you're looking for character witnesses. I'm in Germany, but I'm ready to come to Memphis. I think I can arrange a trip home if you can give me 30 days' notice. I've been awarded the Congressional Medal of Honor, and as soon as I get out of the hospital, I'll be eligible to come home."

Alexander was delighted, to say the least. Trying to hold his composure, he asked, "Are you a Marine?"

"No, sir. Navy SEAL, Team Six. That's all I can say."

"That's fine. That's great. Write me a long letter with everything you remember about Major Armstrong. How did you know him?"

"We were in infiltration teams, Marine and Navy SEAL, in Kuwait. Training and combat. I knew him for over a year. We were inserted behind the Iraqi lines."

"I'll need details, lots of details, about Major Armstrong's character. But I'm interested in your experience, too. How did you earn the Congressional Medal of Honor?"

There was a slight pause. "I was in Afghanistan. I was a lieutenant in charge of a four-man SEAL team. This was my last year. Our mission protocol dictated the killing of anyone discovering the presence of the team during its mission. We came across some local farmers. I made the decision to let the men go free, even though I knew they might alert the local Taliban to our presence, knowing our protocol.

"In a short time, some 100 fighters appeared and engaged our four-man team, wounding all of us and pinning us down in position. A Chinook helicopter sent to rescue our team was hit and destroyed, killing 16 on board. With two dead and one wounded, I crawled to a higher, exposed position to gain radio contact for extraction and support. I was wounded. Barely breathing."

Murphy paused again. When he resumed, his voice sounded somehow thicker.

"I was rescued with one other SEAL. Had I followed my training and procedure and killed those farmers, the loss of the team, rescuers, and equipment may have been avoided."

Alexander could hear the stress in the man's voice. "Let's get you home. We'll talk about it another time," he said.

"Yes, Mr. Alexander." He cleared his throat, and his voice sounded stronger. "Major Armstrong had more character than anyone I've met in the military service. I will help. Frankly, I feel terrible. I don't deserve the medal."

Several days later, a FedEx package arrived. It contained a 20-page handwritten letter and a one-page summary of Lt. Donald Murphy's 16 years of service. He was an "old man," having enlisted in the Navy in 1989 at the age of 18. He was now 34.

His account of Major Armstrong was unbelievable.

Chapter 33

August 10, 2005, Wednesday
Office of John Alexander
Memphis, Tennessee
No defense of intoxication

Alexander was ready for the jury. Hopefully, the judge would rule his defense of Major Armstrong admissible, and he could use his character witnesses. The prosecutor, Mildred Hertond, had filed a motion to block his defense, and the judge would rule on that the morning of trial. He had to have his experts and character witnesses ready for trial, all arrangements made.

Major Armstrong was also ready. He had read the expert affidavits and changed his mind. His lawyer was not crazy. But he was still adamant about one thing. "Remember, no defense of intoxication."

"Gotcha," said Alexander, lying to his client. He didn't intend for his client to make that decision. Alexander would indeed use intoxication as a defense—if he had to.

Chapter 34

August 11, 2005, Thursday
Naval Medical Center
San Diego, California
Semper fi

Navy Lieutenant Murphy had been moved from Germany to the Naval Medical Center, San Diego, California. Alexander decided to fly out and meet him.

"Our job was to get information," Lieutenant Murphy said, as they were eating lunch in the hospital cafeteria. "We were not to torture anyone. We were to get into the mind and heart of our enemy. Scare him. No torture. 'Don't be trigger happy,' Armstrong had warned us. He was the leader of our Navy-Marine Corps infiltration team."

Alexander nodded.

"If captured, we were all supposed to lie that the invasion would come by sea, amphibian. We didn't really know, but we assumed it was a lie. We had all been trained at the Navy and Marine Corps Intelligence Training Center in Virginia. Major Armstrong had also attended the Center for Advanced Operational Culture Learning, called C-A-O-C-L, kay-ah-cul, at Quantico, Virginia. He insisted that knowing the culture of our enemy would be vital to any successful interrogation. That's what he was taught at Quantico, he said.

"He said that the people in Iraq had lived in a world of terror and intimidation for 30-plus years. Threats and intimidation would not be effective.

"I argued both those ideas at first." He smiled, shaking his head. "In my mind, these were not walk-ins, people off the street, or soldiers on the battlefield. We'd have no time to be nice and respectful of their rights. We needed immediate information quickly. Possible ambushes, attacks, improvised explosive devices, convoy security. They were a fanatical and implacable enemy. Get real! We had to be quick and hard on them. They hated us. Despised us. Hated everything we stood for and held dear. They were ruthless, tough, adaptive, willing to do anything to destroy us!

"Armstrong said no. No torture. It was his way, or we were out. He said, 'Decide now, right now.'"

Lieutenant Murphy shook his head and took a big bite of his sandwich. After he'd had a few sips of some very hot black coffee, he said, "No one quit." He shook his head again, and then he laughed.

"You know, he did it. I couldn't believe it. The last time I saw him, he said, '*Semper fi.*' I never dreamed he would live. You see, we were to be inserted in the desert behind enemy lines by helicopter. There were eight Marines and four Navy SEALs. We were all specially trained for this mission. While we were in a bunker behind enemy lines, he made three life-or-death decisions. I never thought he would live through *any* of them, but he did what he had to do to help the other Marines and us.

"The first decision he made was to expose himself to enemy fire while pulling another wounded Marine out of the line of fire. He took more enemy fire, doing this. Once they found enough cover to allow them to assess their wounds, they discovered they each had multiple injuries, but there were only enough life-saving bandages for one.

"Major Armstrong made a second decision and forfeited his medical supplies to the other Marine. Later, he told me that it made more sense to use all of the bandages on one than to split the supplies and have both of them bleed to death.

"In an attempt to flush us from our cover, the enemy tossed a hand grenade. It landed within a few feet of us. Armstrong's selfless decision number three was to use his own severely wounded body to protect us from shrapnel.

He lost at least 40% of his blood from more than 30 shrapnel and six gunshot wounds, but he survived! It was extraordinary heroism. He shielded us and *survived*."

Alexander could tell that though these were hard memories, Murphy wanted to tell his story. The two men ate in companionable silence for a few minutes, and then Murphy quietly resumed.

"Yeah, Armstrong recovered, but he was never the same. It was likely post-traumatic stress disorder. His injuries would force his retirement. I was at the Camp Pendleton ceremony when he was awarded the Navy Cross.

"Anyway, we had radioed our information, and we were told to leave—just as we were surprised by what must have been ten to twelve enemy soldiers carrying automatic weapons and rocket-propelled grenades. It was time to get the hell out of there. We popped smoke. We left our bulletproof vests and scrambled. We carried Armstrong about seven miles in the desert in a Marine poncho.

"It was a 22-hour ordeal. We engaged and shot about 25 enemy soldiers along the way. We moved through the day and the night, resting as necessary. It was the worst day of my life. I'll remember it as long as I live."

Alexander shook his head, not wanting to speak and break Lieutenant Murphy's stream of thought.

"We had AC-130 Spectre gunship support if we needed it. We engaged and neutralized those bastards one by one as we fled to the landing zone. In spite of Armstrong's wounds, our wounds, and bad weather, the Medevac made it, and we made it. Armstrong had great strength of character. He had no fear! He was a leader. We used enemy duct tape from the bunker on his arms and legs to stop bleeding. Duct tape! Can you believe it?"

He laughed.

"We were all wounded, but we all survived. The mission was a success. We had radioed invaluable information on enemy positions and movements. We set up the LZ, the landing zone, to get a Medevac helicopter to land at a designated spot. We had radio contact and GPS.

"One of the soldiers we captured claimed he had lived in the United States. He spoke English. Said he had gone to school at the University of South Carolina. He was a captain and our best source of information. He wanted to go with us, but Armstrong said no. We tied him up and left him in the bunker."

"Hospital Corpsman Second Class, Stanley Philips, a SEAL, worked miracles on all of us. Brandon Miles did much of the carrying. He was a Marine corporal, built like a mule. Another recon Marine, Sergeant Harry Hicks, had been a marksmanship instructor at Parris Island. He was our best sharpshooter.

"Our interpreter was a Marine. He was an American Marine, but also a Sunni Muslim. We all trusted him, fighting to help the people of Iraq and protect his religion. He lived in Columbus, Ohio. His linguistic skills were outstanding. I knew all these guys personally. Now, I don't know where they've gone. Here's a written list with name, rank, serial number of each."

He handed Alexander a piece of paper. Alexander took it and thanked him.

"It was 130 degrees in the day. We were miserable traveling. Some of the enemy soldiers we captured were tired of the violence, the intimidation, murders by their leaders. They talked, just like Armstrong said they would. He was right. It took no torture. If they didn't talk, we just tied them up. Gagged them.

"We don't know what happened to them afterward, but we didn't have to kill or torture a single soldier to get information. All but two talked. We think we got good information. Bridges, ambush points, troop deployments, number of troops here and there. Weapons, ammunition, you name it. There were probably 10,000 troops in our area. We were right in the middle of their formation. We just went out at night and captured them."

"How?" Alexander asked.

"Oh, tricks of the trade, sir. I'll never disclose how you go undetected, like a snake in the sand." For a moment, he paused as if lost in thought.

"CWO-2 Sanders was the best. He must have had American Indian in him. What a character! It was a challenge to him. He carried only a knife. Not a big KA-BAR, just a small, razor-sharp, six-inch blade. The blade would bend if you hit a bone. He said he had to kill two enemy soldiers who resisted so much he couldn't bring them to our bunker."

Alexander detected a light in Murphy's eyes as he remembered the brave men he had fought beside.

"Elvis Winstead, Lance Corporal. What a Marine. He never complained. See the movie *Jarhead?* They had it all wrong. Not much better than the movie *Full Metal Jacket.*"

The two men were done with their meals. Murphy drained the last of his coffee. He nodded his head and sat back in his chair.

"I'm a SEAL. Proud of it. Those Marines were something else. '*Semper fi*' means '*Semper fi,*' nothing more, nothing less. Always faithful. Always loyal. How we all survived is a miracle. Recon Marines are special."

He sighed.

"Navy Petty Officer Second Class Kevin Hall was killed. He was the best SEAL of the team."

Chapter 35

August 12, 2005, Friday morning
Office of John Alexander
Memphis, Tennessee
An inspiration to everyone

Alexander was in his office early. He had a 9:00 a.m. appointment set up with Alec Henderson, who was one of the Airborne Rangers looking for a downed Black Hawk pilot in Nicaragua, Central America, with Major Armstrong in 1983.

Ann buzzed him. "Alec Henderson is ready to see you."

Alexander welcomed the man into his office. "Good morning, Alec," he said, shaking his hand. "Coffee?"

Henderson politely accepted. Alexander served him and took a cup for himself. The two men sat comfortably, and after a couple of minutes of cordial conversation, Alexander began the interview.

"Now what about your military experience?"

"I enlisted in the Army out of high school. My older brother was in the Army, and he talked me into it. 'Go airborne,' he said. I did. After basic training at Ft. Benning, Georgia, I completed airborne training and Ranger School. I was sent straight to Viet Nam. It was 1970.

"I was a member of a hunter-killer team in Viet Nam, and we used a helicopter to investigate an enemy site in some caves near the ocean. While following a trail, we hovered over the edge of a large boulder and came upon a Vietnamese man hiding along the edge of a rock. Dressed in shirt and shorts, he was unarmed and not moving. Simply lying on his back looking up at me.

"The pilot was screaming in my headset, 'Kill him! KILL HIM!' I yelled back that he was unarmed. In those long seconds, I did as was expected. Later that day, after the infantry was inserted to search the complex, I was credited with four more 'kills,' including one who was thought to be a prostitute. Most were the result of blind fire into openings or explosives dropped into them.

"From a documentary, I think it was on the History Channel, I remember that during the World War II battle for the Arnhem Bridge in the Netherlands, a German soldier recounted his experience in the house-to-house battle.

"He said that upon descending the stairs into the basement of one building, he prepared to toss a grenade into a room. Just as he prepared to pull the pin, he heard moaning coming from the room. When he peered around the corner into the room, he found it full of wounded British paratroopers. His comment was that had he thrown the grenade into that room of defenseless men, he would not be able to enjoy the nights' rest he is able to now enjoy.

"Know what I mean?" He took a deep breath. "I was an Airborne Ranger in the elite 82nd Airborne Division, and now, after less than 30 days combat service, I was beginning to doubt my actions."

"More coffee?" Alexander asked him.

"Yes, sir. Thank you."

"You retired from the Army in 1990. Twenty years of service. Is that correct?"

"Yes, I retired as a sergeant major. I live in North Carolina now—not far from Ft. Bragg. I remember Major Armstrong very well. Haven't seen him since we left Central America in 1983."

"Well, Alec, tell me what happened."

"Willie Armstrong was a new Marine lieutenant. We were in the jungles of Central America. God knows where. Supposedly Nicaragua. We were searching for a Black Hawk pilot who was the sole survivor of a crash into the jungle. Armstrong was our leader. We were just regular

155

Army grunts—Airborne Rangers. Well trained, but this was our first mission in the jungles of Central America.

"We came to a village that was deserted. A horse had been attacked and savagely eaten by something. It was a mess. We crept on. It was a dark and moonless night. Suddenly, two natives slipped out of the jungle growth onto our path, directly in front.

"They told us they had seen a man-eating, giant crocodile, over 20 feet in length. The villagers had fled. The crocodile had attacked a horse. They were returning to their village. No sign of the pilot, but they had heard the helicopter crash to the north, near the river. They said there were many bandits or terrorist bands roaming the area.

"A few miles away we came to the river, and Lieutenant Armstrong stepped into the current. We followed, in a line. There was a big splash in the water. We ran, retreating back down the path—all but Lieutenant Armstrong, who turned around, followed us, and shouted. We stopped on his orders.

"He marched us back up the path, across the river, around and back across the river, and around and back across the river. Then he ordered us to fall out and clean our weapons, ready for inspection. It was mind boggling! He re-established his authority. Great example of the kind of leader he became."

He paused, then took a deep breath.

"Two Marines were killed later that year in a terrorist ambush. Those months I spent with Armstrong in that jungle I never forgot. No man has more courage or leadership ability. He was as black as the ace of spades. He was an inspiration to everyone who served with or around him. A perfect example of dignity, grace, and great skill. Most of all, moral and honest.

"I never lost my courage again. I never forgot that damn crocodile or Lieutenant Armstrong. I had spent a tour in Viet Nam, but I was a scared man, scared. He wasn't.'"

Henderson was silent for a few minutes. Finally, he smiled and continued.

"We were near Juan Venado Island, near Las Peñitas, Nicaragua. Very beautiful beaches. No one lived on the island. Las Peñitas was a small fishing village with a mangrove forest. Lots of birds, crabs, turtles, and...crocodiles! Beyond this forest is where we had come upon the story of the *big* crocodile." He laughed.

"But I was worried about the bandits and jaguars. Jaguars were the Western Hemisphere's largest feline and the third largest cat in the world. I had encountered a tiger in Viet Nam. He was carrying away Airborne Rangers *alive* until we tracked him down and shot him—I mean her. It was a female. The roar of a jaguar? It's more like a cough. It will scare the hell out of you! We never found the pilot."

Henderson set down his coffee cup. He seemed a bit tired, but he didn't complain. He continued.

"My father was a Marine. In 1941, he was captured on Guam by the Japanese. He spent four years as a prisoner of war in three different prisons. He was liberated at Suguro Prison Camp. He became a real estate appraiser for the Federal Housing Administration and retired after 30 years of service. I was born in Van Buren, Arkansas. Do you know where that is?"

"I sure do," replied Alexander. "Alec, can you come back for trial? I want you to be a character witness for Major Armstrong. You know about the killing, my letter?"

"Yes, sir. Major Armstrong's character and credibility is beyond question. I'll be there. Just call me."

"My secretary, Ann, will make your travel arrangements at our expense. We'll call you."

Henderson was a remarkable person. There was something about him that Alexander really liked.

Chapter 36

August 12, 2005, Friday afternoon
Office of John Alexander
Memphis, Tennessee
A man of honesty and courage

Later that afternoon, Alexander began to read the resumes of the other potential character witnesses who had served with Armstrong. One stood out. He was another Airborne Ranger who had also retired as a sergeant major. He lived in Kentucky. Alexander looked through the resume and attached letter.

Sergeant Major George Rowe had an impressive career. He, too, was a Viet Nam veteran, and he'd been a team sergeant of the 5th Special Forces Group. Armstrong had enlisted in the Marine Corps in 1976, at the age of 18. He'd completed the Army Rangers program and later became a Marine lieutenant. In the late 1970s, Rowe had spent a lot of time as a sergeant with Armstrong. They had both worked in a secret, special forces training program in North Carolina.

In 1982, Rowe had been hand-picked to set up the Survival, Evasion, Resistance, and Escape (SERE) program at the Army's Special Warfare Center and School. Back then, the school was called U.S. Army John F. Kennedy Special Warfare Center (SWC). The name had been changed three years later.

Rowe had spent the last seven years at the Special Warfare Center as the Phase 1 instructor of the Special Forces Basic Enlisted Division. He had personally written every lesson plan, set up a jungle-training program, and wrote the RECORDS course.

What's that? Alexander thought.

Rowe remembered a training exercise in which he was playing possum, laying in a ditch. In his letter, he described the incident.

Armstrong was told I was dead. He poked me hard with a real bayonet, and I moved. He cut me! Boy, was I pissed off. They grabbed me and held me down while I was searched, and then they tied me up and took me prisoner.

Good thing. I would have knocked that "nigger's" head off. I told him so. Called him a black son-of-a-bitch. He took it with a smile. We became friends. I've spent hours talking to him.

His character is beyond question.

I'll come any time, any place. Just call me.

George Rowe
Sergeant Major, U.S. Army retired

After Armstrong got his commission, Rowe lost track of him until Major Armstrong returned from Iraq in 1992. A P.S. on Rowe's letter added that he had seen a lot of men in action, under fire, attacked by overwhelming Viet Cong force. He would pick Armstrong over any man he had ever met to stand beside him under fire. A man of honesty and courage.

Alexander now had three good character witnesses. He needed another. Or did he? He had all the names and identities he needed. Should there be a fourth? Who would it be?

Chapter 37

August 15, 2005, Monday
Office of John Alexander
Memphis, Tennessee
How do you prove it?

"Mr. Alexander. I think I know Major Armstrong better than anyone. Trust me. We were together night and day, for three years. When do you want me to come? Set it up. I'm in Vancouver."

After the phone call, Alexander hung up and began to think about the situation. This potential character witness, John "Andrew" McKenzie, was from Oregon. He had a Ph.D. in political science from the University of British Columbia. He said he'd taught there and had lectured at Harvard and Yale. He taught at the London School of Economics as a professor of political sociology. What a witness he would be!

Armstrong and McKenzie had both enlisted in the Marines in 1976, and along with Bruce Voltz, they served together in Sicily as security guards at a nuclear weapons facility. These were nuclear torpedoes for submarines and nuclear bombs for Navy and Marine aircraft. They were later transferred to the 4th Marines at Camp Pendleton, California.

In 1991, when a U.S.-led coalition drove Iraqi forces from Kuwait, ending the Persian Gulf War, Major Armstrong was there. So was John McKenzie.

Alexander already had three outstanding character witnesses. Should he add a fourth? What evidence to use as proof was an art and a science. Too much and you could irritate the jury. Not enough, and you could lose the case! He

160

had to make the right decision. He decided he would use all four, and he would not need any others.

Next, he would concentrate on expert witnesses, get affidavits, and then he'd be ready to convince the judge to accept his amygdala defense. He needed an expert molecular neurobiologist and an expert on language. If "nigger" is the most offensive word in the English language, how do you prove it?

Brain scans and expert opinion evidence, he said to himself. *What else?*

Chapter 38

August 22, 2005, Monday
Office of the Dyersburg State Gazette
Dyersburg, Tennessee
It was just a rumor

Alexander drove from Memphis to Dyersburg, Tennessee, to investigate the execution of Armstrong's father. At the *Dyersburg State Gazette* newspaper office on Highway 51, he obtained a photo of the killing from the editor, George Stone. It had been published in the paper. KKK, horses, the crowd of angry citizens. Armstrong's father had been accused of the rape of a white girl and burned to death in public without a trial.

"No one was ever prosecuted for the crime," the editor said. "Our sheriff was the type of man who got confessions out of people by putting them naked on a 50-pound block of ice. The man was on the ice block in the basement of the jail for eight hours, according to rumor. I was ordered not to print that. It was 'just a rumor.'"

"Did you believe it?"

"Yes, I did. But I couldn't afford to lose my job. I became and remained the editor because I knew when to keep my mouth shut and my pen in my pocket."

"Thanks, Mr. Stone. I'll need your affidavit, without the rumors, of course. Just tell us about the photo and your article, okay?"

He nodded. "Yes."

On the way back to Memphis, Alexander tried to imagine what it was like to be burned alive. It was beyond his imagination.

Chapter 39

August 23, 2005, Tuesday
Highway 7 toward Memphis
Lafayette County, Mississippi
Clyde Rose

It was three o'clock in the morning, and Clyde Rose was on his way back to San Francisco, California, from the small southern town of Oxford, Mississippi, where he had attended an annual family reunion. It was quite dark as he traveled along Highway 7 toward Memphis.

As he came over the last hill approaching the Tallahatchie River Bridge, just inside Lafayette County, he was met by a blast of automobile headlights. He proceeded slowly, feeling the apprehension that most blacks experienced in Mississippi creep over his body and through his mind. He wondered if this could be the police, or what, and he was afraid.

It was a roadblock.

At the roadblock, he was met with the stern face of Mississippi Highway Patrol Trooper Paul Robin, who motioned for him to leave the roadway. He was questioned on the side of the highway with a bright flashlight beam in his face.

"Do you have a driver's license?"

"Yes."

"Let me see it." The trooper took his time scrutinizing the card. "California? Hmm. What're you doin' around here, boy?"

"I've been visiting my family over the Fourth of July holidays in Oxford."

"Whose car are you driving? Do you have registration papers?" The trooper started to shine his flashlight toward the passenger front seat of the car.

"Yes."

"Let me see them."

Clyde knew to retrieve the papers slowly from the glove box. He handed them over.

The officer read out loud, "Marvin Holden."

"Yes, he's a friend. I borrowed the car after I flew from San Francisco to Memphis to come down here for a few days and go back to Memphis."

"Is this the same Marvin Holden with the paper company in Memphis?"

"Sure, that's him. Do you know him?"

"Alright. Just sit here a few minutes. We'll have some more questions."

The trooper motioned to other troopers at the side of the road, one of whom reached for his mobile radio. Fifteen minutes later, members of the Mississippi Bureau of Narcotics arrived.

They began to question Clyde further, and shortly thereafter a narcotic-sniffing dog from the Parchman Penitentiary arrived. At first, Clyde was unaware of the dog, but after he had consented to a search of his vehicle, the searching officer wanted permission to search his clothing bag. He did not consent.

"Well, we'll just have to use the dog."

Clyde never liked dogs, and he certainly didn't like the looks of this dog—an aggressive black Labrador. He overheard some of the men referring to the dog's name, "J.D.," for Jack Daniel's. As the dog began to jump in the car and nose his way around, Clyde knew he was now in trouble.

One of the officers grabbed a bag, took it out, unzipped it, and searched the inside a suit coat pocket. He found a small package and opened it. Soon, eleven smaller packages of snow-white powder wrapped in cellophane-like material were exposed to the various flashlights sweeping across the rear of the trunk.

"Where did you get this?" the officer asked Clyde.

He replied, "I don't wish to make any further statements. I'd like to call my lawyer."

The man laughed. "Put him in the car, boys, and take him to Oxford County Jail. He'll get to call his lawyer when we get ready. Smart nigger. He'll pay for wanting to see that lawyer."

Clyde thought to himself as he rode along, handcuffed, that he certainly was going to pay either way. He had learned since leaving Oxford and living a more sophisticated life in California, that it was not to his advantage to talk to police officers. He wished his lawyer was there right now, so he could go over this entire mess and find some way out.

Chapter 40

August 26, 2005, Friday
Office of John Alexander
Memphis, Tennessee
A big technical difference

Three days later, after having been released from jail on one hundred thousand dollars bond, Clyde Rose went to Memphis, where he visited a lawyer recommended to him by his good friend, Marvin Holden, whose car he had borrowed.

He was not able to see the lawyer immediately, because he was working on another case, but the office secretary had asked Clyde to wait, and she said she would call him as soon as the lawyer was free. She did, and he was now sitting face to face with John Alexander.

Alexander sat there looking at the face of a young black man, a face he had seen many times before. The same expression, those same eyes, and he wondered how so many young men and women could fall prey to cocaine. He preferred whiskey, which, as his criminal defense lawyer friend Wayne Payne had often said, was just as dangerous. Why one was legal and the other illegal baffled them both.

In any event, cocaine was a controlled substance under federal and state laws. He knew he would have his hands full in the State of Mississippi, particularly since Clyde was black. There may have been a Civil War, and there may have been a host of Supreme Court decisions after the Civil War, as well as the Fourteenth Amendment that ensured all citizens equal protection under the laws—but that didn't change the fact that jurors in 2005 were still not color blind.

Blacks in Mississippi, as well as in most of the South, weren't going to be treated fairly by jurors. They were going to be treated differently. Alexander could not wait until he was retired and forgot about all this. He didn't have much time for this case. He had to retire. But how could he say no?

"Mr. Rose, I'll be happy to represent you. It's just a matter of money. Can you pay a retainer fee? I'm very busy right now, but I'll try to work you in."

"How much?"

"Well, Clyde, what kind of work do you do?"

"I work for an LNG Marine tanker company in Oregon. I've got a good job, but I don't have any cash."

"Well, you know, criminal defense lawyers require large retainers, so somehow or other, you're going to have to pay a substantial retainer."

"I'll make the arrangements. How much?"

"Ten thousand dollars."

"I'll get it. I know you're a good lawyer, and I don't want to go to prison."

"Well, I can't guarantee you won't be imprisoned, but I will guarantee your rights will be protected. And if there is any way out of this mess, we'll find it. It seems to me, right off, that the Fourth Amendment to the United States Constitution regarding search and seizure was violated, as well as the Constitution of Mississippi in the same regard."

"What does that mean?"

"Well, if I'm right, it means the evidence—the cocaine—is inadmissible, and that means you can't go back to jail legally. It doesn't mean the judge will agree with me, nor does it mean the Mississippi Supreme Court will agree. Appeals in Mississippi go straight from the trial court to the Mississippi Supreme Court."

"Is that good?"

"Well, I think Mississippi has a reputation for being very protective of the Fourth Amendment. More so than Tennessee or Alabama, and probably as much as California or Oregon."

"Well, I'll leave it up to you. I'll get the money. Just get me out of this mess."

"Let me ask you one last question. Where did you get the cocaine?"

"I bought it from a person I didn't know who was standing on the street in a housing project in Oxford."

Alexander thought for a moment, and while he wanted to know more about this case, he knew he had no business knowing too much. But violating one of his standard rules, he asked, "What were you intending to do with the cocaine?"

"Take it back and use it myself. I bought it for myself."

"You didn't intend to sell the cocaine?"

"No. That's the truth, Mr. Alexander. That's the truth."

There was a big technical difference in the penalty, and both of them knew that. Alexander didn't even have to suggest the answer.

"Okay. Get your money, have it to me in a few days, and then you can depend on me. Remember, without a fee, I can't represent you."

The young black man stood up, shook Alexander's hand, and left the office.

Alexander sat there thinking to himself that this was not a drug trafficker, but just another human caught in a vicious web of circumstances. He had to make a good argument under the Fourth Amendment and hope. At least if he went to trial before he went before the white jury in Mississippi, he had a chance.

He would argue the cocaine was for Clyde's personal use. Being a case of simple possession as opposed to possession with intent to sell or deliver, both felonies in Mississippi, made a difference. The penalties everywhere differed greatly if the user possessed only for personal use as opposed to possession for sale or delivery to others.

Mississippi was no exception. Instead of eight or twenty years, he might be able to squeeze through with three or less or maybe even probation, and if the technical defenses were good, Clyde Rose would never serve another day in jail or prison for this felony.

Chapter 41

August 30, 2005, Tuesday
Lafayette County Courthouse
Oxford, Mississippi
So many good young men

Motions had been filed for some time, and Alexander had received his fee and spent it, as it had been a non-refundable retainer. He drove up to the Lafayette County Courthouse in Oxford, Mississippi. It was a beautifully preserved antebellum building, and it stood out all by itself in the courthouse square.

The day, a steamy hot Tuesday, reminded him of a Tennessee Williams play—and William Faulkner, who had grown up in the area. Faulkner may have been a greater writer than Hemingway, he thought, but how could anyone live a private life in this place? Everything was public. *The Oxford Eagle* had already blasted and convicted his client, and surely the judge and most of the citizens of the country had read the articles.

Oxford was a historic town with many beautiful old buildings reminiscent of the pre-Civil War days of the South. It was the home of the University of Mississippi, and there were many intellectuals in the Oxford area that had come from everywhere, not just Mississippi.

It was a splendid town in many regards, but as he walked up the steps, he knew he was in for a fight. His client was black, and black still meant trouble in the South. *No defense lawyer in the South who is unaware of the color of his client is a good defense lawyer*, he repeated to himself.

The prosecutor at the motion hearing put on his proof in a characteristically good manner, well aware of the issue. His Honor, the trial judge, old, bespectacled, and honored Judge

170

Otto Brown, who had lived his entire life in Oxford, listened carefully, attentively. At the close of the hearing, he ruled in favor of the State with the comment, "Mr. Alexander, this is a close question, but I'm going to deny your motion. If your client is convicted, we can take the matter up post-trial, and of course, as you know, you can appeal this issue to the Supreme Court of Mississippi. Perhaps that's where it ought to be settled anyway."

Alexander turned around, motioned for his client and his client's elderly parents to come along, and they left the courtroom. Standing on the steps of the courthouse, he explained again to the mother and father, both in their eighties, what all this meant, as he had in his office the day before. Just as Clyde had reacted, it seemed to mean nothing to them. All they really wanted to know was whether their son was going to go back to jail.

"Clyde, you're going to have to stand trial. I'm going to let you tell your story to the judge. If they believe you, we can beat the big charge, and you'll be convicted of a lesser included offense. That being the case, the most I think you can get out of this is three, maybe five years, maybe probation and no jail. If you're convicted of anything, we'll appeal it, and we've got a good chance on appeal.

"You heard the trooper's testimony. It's not identical to yours, but it's close enough that we've got our foot in the door. The State at the hearing should have called the dog handler. They didn't. So we can argue that the credentials of the dog as well as those of the handler were not established, and the warrantless search of your car was invalid for this reason as well as the other reasons I've outlined to you. You know, the illegal roadblock, the illegal detention, and most important, that this roadblock was an illegal pretext."

He explained. "These men had all met in the Mississippi Bureau of Narcotics Office prior to setting up the roadblock. The dog handler from the prison was there. The federal DEA agent. You heard them say they had a list of names they were looking for, and the Bureau of Narcotics Agents were flushing out the local bars by going in and walking around, knowing a lot of people would just get up and flee and they would be caught on the highway.

"This is what we call a pretext. There is Mississippi law for our position, and I feel very good about this case. I cannot imagine it won't be reversed if you're convicted. Does that make sense?"

"Well, Mr. Alexander, I'm not sure I understand you fully, but if you're saying there's a chance I won't go to jail, just keep fighting. I like the way you operate. I'm proud of you, and if I have to go to prison, I'll know I was defended properly. I can come up with money if there is more fee due."

Clyde's parents, looking bewildered, limped off with their son. The three of them got into their old pickup truck. As Alexander watched them drive out of the square and down the street, he wondered what type of home they lived in, and he felt more convinced than ever that it was his duty to win this case.

If only this young man and the millions of others like him did not crave this crazy white powder, he wouldn't even be here. What if Wayne was right? If people really could be genetically altered to not even desire the stuff…if they didn't want cocaine like humans don't want to eat sand and gravel (as he had heard Wayne say so many times), there wouldn't be a necessity for controlled substance laws.

Young men like Clyde and old folks like his parents would not be enduring these ordeals. A world turned upside down. Would it be better or worse? What would happen to all the people who depended upon the criminal justice system for income arising out of the prosecution of such felons?

On the sixty-mile return drive from Oxford to Memphis, Alexander kept thinking about all the young men he had met and known as a lawyer—particularly the black young men who were into using or selling crack cocaine. It was a way out. A way to get expensive jewelry, cars, clothing, women, power…and there was no other way out.

It wasn't just the kick from the cocaine itself that was a problem. It was a way for people to obtain large sums of money. These people had no education. They had no training. Alexander had often heard white, southern adults argue how getting jobs was the answer to the problem with blacks.

It seemed so simplistic. He knew a job was hard to find, and the mental state of mind of these young people was quite different from those who so easily criticized. As so often is the case, many of the people so quick to criticize had never really worked a day in their lives. They lived off their father's money or their inheritance or their spouse's income or their luck. Luck played such an important part in life.

There were those who were lucky and those who were unlucky, and there were those who had means and there were those who didn't. As one lawyer put it, the question was whether you were going to be somebody who had something, or somebody who didn't have something.

Certainly, the roads and paths of different humans were quite different. Citizens were not created equal, nor were their environments or life experiences the same. Alexander reminded himself that when the Declaration of Independence was written, "all men were created equal" meant men, not women nor blacks. It referred to colonial American *males*. Thomas Jefferson had a very narrow idea in mind.

As he continued on down the road, Alexander remembered another case involving a black man and a Corvette automobile with the personalized tag "Snow White"—and how the young man had been convicted. He had unsuccessfully defended him in federal court in Memphis and had even appealed the case to Cincinnati and the Sixth Circuit unsuccessfully. That was also a case of illegal search and seizure, and a violation of the Fourth Amendment. It was an illegal dog sniff case, too.

And then there was the dog sniff case of Melvin Norton and the packages mailed by Federal Express from San Diego to Memphis. Another case of the illegal use of warrants and dogs. Those dogs had names he couldn't remember. He was getting old. His memory was failing. It was indeed time to retire. His mind leap-frogged from one case to another as he drove up the highway.

Ten years ago, Alexander had defended Marvin Holden, the man who had recommended Alexander to Clyde as a good lawyer who could be trusted. Marvin had been arrested after almost half a million dollars in cash had been seized in a bank account by IRS agents, as well as an Excalibur, several Mercedes automobiles, and various other automobiles. A total of nine houses were also seized, all to become the subject of federal civil and criminal forfeiture proceedings in Mississippi.

Marvin had gotten out of jail on two hundred thousand dollars bail and had posted bail with a corporate surety when he came to Alexander's office for advice. Alexander represented him at the bail hearing. He recalled their conversation, remembering it as if it were only yesterday.

"Marvin, you know you told me you'd given up this cocaine business years ago. Don't you remember? After I represented you in the seizure case with the twenty-five thousand dollars under the carpet?" It had been more than ten years ago since that case, but this was the Marvin Holden who had loaned Clyde a car! Was there a conflict of interest?

"Yes, Mr. Alexander," Marvin had said. "I quit. I haven't been dealing in cocaine since then."

"Well, then, what's all this about cocaine, houses, millions of dollars, Excaliburs, and Mercedes?"

"Well, it's true, they're mine. But I'm telling you, I never dealt in drugs in Mississippi, and I haven't dealt in any drugs since that case, Mr. Alexander."

"Do you swear, Marvin, the charges are not true?"

As if that was important.

"I do."

"Then I can represent you. I believe you."

It really didn't matter to Alexander. Guilty or not, Marvin was entitled to the effective assistance of counsel under the Sixth Amendment.

But now he had Clyde's case to try before a jury and on appeal with the Mississippi Supreme Court. If Clyde went to trial, Marvin Holden's name, identity, and unlawful drug business might become an issue. Clyde might be convicted as a drug dealer. Alexander was worried.

Alexander knew Marvin had a legitimate job and legitimate businesses. His money came from those legitimate businesses. Yes, he had been accused of engaging in a continuing criminal enterprise, a conspiracy—or a kind of conspiracy—but that was years ago.

"There's no truth, no truth to it!" Marvin had said. "I've never dealt drugs in Mississippi. Frankly, I'm too scared to. I don't believe anybody is treated fairly in Mississippi, and I sure don't want to run afoul of those people in Oxford. My being black, you know, and you know, my girlfriend, Clarice. She's white."

Alexander wondered where all this was going to lead and what a tangle it already was. He was concerned about ethics and conflicts of interest, and those things that are pitfalls for criminal defense lawyers. Collecting his fee was also in the back of his mind. He certainly didn't want to run afoul of any money laundering charges or those things prosecutors love to delve into with defense lawyers. The only thing a prosecutor liked to do better than to convict clients was convict their lawyers. He was well aware of this.

As Alexander continued his drive home that evening, he kept thinking to himself, *How could so many good young men get involved in this illegal drug business?*

With few exceptions, all the drug traffickers he had known would have made good soldiers or Marines, good infantrymen. The kind of people you would want beside you in a really tough battle.

And he thought about the Marine Corps, particularly Iwo Jima. Those nights when the Marines were in holes and the only connection was a piece of string tied from one arm to the other from hole to hole so they could signal each other when danger lurked. He thought about all those nights Marines spent there, waiting for the Japanese to infiltrate, each thinking this night would be his last. The night on Iwo Jima when his uncle lost his right arm to a Japanese major's sword, and how another Marine had shot the major in the face with a forty-five pistol. The major had fallen into his hole. That blood. It was two weeks before he could get a bath.

Alexander could smell the blood, like the smell of blood when he almost lost his life in Viet Nam in that French cemetery. He could feel the pain. He now began to relive that experience—not remember, but relive. He became very frightened. It was pitch black. He needed medical treatment. His left hand was badly injured, and he would later lose fingers.

Suddenly, he snapped awake. He had almost run off the highway.

He concentrated on his driving. It had begun to rain. He would have been proud to have served with any of these drug trafficking men, and he felt all of them would have been dependable fighting men. Well, not all of them. Some would have been cowards. Some would have retreated. Some would not have been heroes. Even the Marine Corps failed with some men. How could this be? It had to be genetics. The answer, the secret, had to be locked in the genes.

The next morning at 11 o'clock, he was to be back in Memphis federal court to report the status of another new case to His Honor. Doug Barnes, also known as Mark Halloway, was charged with conspiracy to sell two kilograms of cocaine. How could this be? Mark had been the best cooperating individual in the history of the Western District of Tennessee, and now he was facing federal imprisonment of over two hundred months.

Chapter 42

August 31, 2005, Wednesday
Office of U.S. Assistant Attorney Fred Massey
Memphis, Tennessee
Mark Halloway

At 9:00 a.m., Alexander sat in the office of the assistant United States attorney, Fred Massey, and listened to the FBI agents explain the trap they had set for Mark and why.

He couldn't believe it.

"Were you trying to catch Deputy Sheriff Snow?" he asked. "Or were you trying to catch Mark?"

Mark had been working for Deputy Snow, an FBI narcotics agent. Alexander suspected these FBI agents were jealous of his success and were trying to discredit him.

"Mark, of course," the agent replied. "We had no reason to be after Snow."

"It seems to me," said Alexander, "from the nature of the investigation and the way it was handled—not letting Snow know what you were doing—that you were thinking he was involved."

Massey shook his head. "No, we never considered him. We just felt as good investigators we should totally control this investigation ourselves."

"So, you say there was no jealousy on your part about the fact that last year alone, Snow's work resulted in more arrests, more seizures, more automobiles, more everything than the entire local office of the FBI?"

"Who said that?"

"I know it's a fact, and you know it's a fact," Alexander responded, becoming weary of the game.

"But who said it? What authority?"

"I'm saying it."

The agents stared angrily at Alexander.

Alexander turned to address the assistant U.S. attorney.

"Fred, is this the truth? Is this the way it went down? You were there. Did Mark admit he was buying cocaine to resell?"

"Yes."

"But he tells me his intentions were to set this man up for Officer Snow, and he was being paid a thousand dollars a kilogram for this work."

"That's true, Alexander. But unfortunately, as Agent Sullivan has explained, we think Mark has gone bad. You know, when we worked out of the last deal on his bank robberies and the drug trafficking, I told you I was skeptical he would be able to survive without returning to his criminal way of life. And you remember we discussed whether he was a genetic defect under your crazy theory."

"Yeah, I think he's a defect, but I *don't* think he's guilty of what you guys are accusing him of this time, and I'm refusing to accept it."

"Well, let a jury decide."

Alexander shook his head. "You know I can't let a jury decide this case. I can't even trust the judge, and I don't know a better judge than His Honor Judge Scott. It's just not human to ask one man to judge another in these circumstances."

He paused.

"I don't mean it's not human. I mean it's not possible for humans to judge honestly in this situation. It's just too much prejudicial information. You know, the bank robberies and the million-dollar drug traffic deals, despite all the cooperation."

They sat looking at each other. The agents and the prosecutor knew Alexander was trapped. He had no other alternative but to plead Mark guilty, again—and under the federal guidelines, *there* was a real problem.

Alexander finally spoke.

"Okay, you guys, let's say you got him. What's the best deal?"

"There is no deal," said Massey.

"There's got to be a deal. I can't go in there under the guidelines. You've got to do something."

"There's no deal. You plead guilty and go to the judge under the guidelines."

"I'm not going to. We'll set it for trial. Thanks for your time. I know I've imposed on all of you. I appreciate it very much." He stood up.

"Oh, Alexander, you know Mark's special and important to me, too," Massey said. "He did us a lot of good work, and we haven't forgotten. If there were any way…. But, you know, Sullivan is the case agent. If I were going to change my mind, you'd have to change his, first."

"Thanks. See you."

Alexander walked down the hall briskly. Not only was he mad at the agents and the assistant U.S. attorney, but he was mad at his client for such a stupid set of circumstances. He wondered what the truth was, and he couldn't help but think maybe this time Mark wasn't really disclosing everything. He knew darn good and well the agents and the attorney were not disclosing everything.

Truth. What an illusion. He knew truth wasn't the goal of the criminal justice system in the first place. No matter what Supreme Court judges said, or textbook writers, or philosophers, the goal of adversaries in the criminal justice system was to win. A prosecutor wanted to win on behalf of the State or the government, and more so for himself. The defense lawyers wanted to win on behalf of the defendant and for themselves. It was just a matter of winning. It was a battle of wits.

The government was not going to win the war against drugs. There was no way to win, and he knew the day he died, unless something really, really dramatic happened, things would be just as bad—there would be billions of dollars worth of cocaine being sold. And millions of users and thousands of dealers. And that Peru, Bolivia, and Colombia would continue to produce cocaine. And it would somehow get to the United States. And there was no stopping the supply, even if you took the dastardly step of using the military, as in real war.

Oh, what a mistake it would be to get the military involved in such a fight, he thought. But if he were being completely honest, he couldn't blame the government for considering such an alternative. Crime had become the nation's number one problem, and the nation was about to be swallowed by it.

Addiction was really society's biggest problem—bigger than the war in Iraq! Communism, terrorists, nuclear war, and overpopulation just didn't seem like very big problems now. Cocaine, murder, burglary, and rape were the kind of real problems facing this nation, and the only solution, he thought, was genetic engineering.

Chemical addiction had to be stopped using scientific methods—not punishment or phony rehabilitation schemes. How could he put all this together? He was just a nobody, but he remembered Robert F. Kennedy's statement in his Day of Affirmation Address in South Africa in 1966, about how a tiny ripple of hope can become a "current which can sweep down the mightiest walls of oppression and resistance." Could he be the first tiny ripple and bring about an end to drug trafficking? All major crime?

He fell asleep that night with Kennedy's words ringing in his ears, and as he dreamed he could see large ripples of water. As they moved out, a giant wave rose, sinking all the ships in its way and destroying islands and all in its path.

What started the little ripple? he asked himself the next morning, as he sat alone eating his breakfast. What a senseless war society was fighting against crime. There was no way to win. This was like Viet Nam, and he represented the enemy! Mark had entered a guilty plea, and he and Mark would throw themselves on the mercy of His Honor.

If things went badly, Mark would be in prison, not Alexander. *Thank God*, he thought.

Chapter 43

September 1, 2005, Thursday
Office of John Alexander
Memphis, Tennessee
Trustworthy, honest, courageous

Alexander could no longer be distracted by any other new cases. He just couldn't. He had to stop, retire. He was angry at himself about this.

But the Armstrong case was shaping up. Armstrong's character witnesses were marvelous. Never before had he heard so much praise. Each person had said beyond question that Armstrong was a man of character, trustworthy, honest, courageous. And these men were well respected, themselves.

Two weeks ago, he thought he would only need four character witnesses, but Alexander had recently spent an hour with retired sergeant major Curtis Newhouse, the Army Airborne Ranger he had spoken with on the phone back in June.

It was the ambush in Central America of Newhouse and others, including Bruce Voltz, that had grabbed Alexander's attention. Armstrong had risked his life to save other men he hardly knew—Army Airborne Rangers, Marines, and a Navy SEAL—all white men. In the ambush, he was the only black in the fight. He had to fight off the attackers, as the others were unable to move because of heavy machine gun fire and automatic weapons.

It was night, pitch dark. They had recovered a weapons cache and were returning to their jungle base when the well-planned ambush had stopped their egress. One of the Rangers had been hit in his right femoral artery by machine gun fire that had come from both sides of the road. Armstrong had acted quickly and put a tourniquet on the man's leg. A Marine sergeant was killed, and the others returned the fire.

Usually a firefight lasted from five seconds to five minutes. This one lasted four hours. Major Armstrong was in charge and inspired the others by his leadership and bravery. Before he slid off into the darkness, he whispered to his fellow Marines, "*Semper fidelis.*"

Curtis Newhouse had details. "After sustaining minor wounds to an arm and both legs from exploding mortar rounds, Armstrong charged a four-man enemy team setting up an RPG (rocket-propelled grenade) position. With complete disregard for his own safety, Armstrong charged the position with a rifle and hand grenade. He fell only *after* he had killed two of the insurgents, wounded a third, and disrupted the enemy force. The enemy fled!"

Armstrong's platoon cleared the area with a counterattack. Armstrong was evacuated by helicopter to a military hospital, where he recovered.

Alexander by now had learned that throughout his military career, Major Armstrong had been awarded more than a Silver Star and a Purple Heart for his actions. He'd been awarded a Bronze Star with combat "V", as well as the Navy Cross and other medals. Only the Medal of Honor was higher than Armstrong's decorations.

How could a man with so much honor and service to his country face life in prison for murder? It didn't seem right. His military record was the best and most impressive Alexander had ever seen.

There were now five character witnesses, and they were all outstanding. In his entire career, Alexander had never had such character witnesses—but this was because Armstrong was a "man's man." Alexander had never represented such a man.

Chapter 44

September 6, 2005, Tuesday
Office of John Alexander
Memphis, Tennessee
The basis of criminal defense

The Sequatchie Valley of Tennessee was part of the Cumberland Plateau, and cutting through the center of the valley was the Sequatchie River. This was coal country. So, when confronted with a new case that September morning, the day after Labor Day, a new client accused of selling worthless coal mines in Sequatchie County, Tennessee, Alexander became intrigued.

He agreed to visit the county and the coal mine sites and to consider representing in the United States District Court in Memphis, Tennessee, David Hill, the man accused of the heinous crime known as RICO—the Racketeer Influenced and Corrupt Organization Act, Title IX of the Organized Crime Control Act of 1970.

How was he going to retire if he kept this up?

RICO had become the "darling" of federal prosecutors. Federal courts were very different than state courts, because federal prosecutors got away with more cheating—cheating defendants, insisting they were only performing their duty as federal prosecutors. Most of them believed if the defendant was guilty, it was alright to cheat—another kind of "ends justify the means" mentality.

In fact, Alexander had come to recognize that "the end justifies the means" was the basis for the criminal justice system. It was really the philosophical underpinnings for all the players in the system, even criminal defense lawyers who had come to recognize that if the government could cheat and win, the defendant had to try to cheat and win!

185

This RICO case now had 20 defendants and a proposed trial which could last six months. He knew this mega-trial monster in and of itself would result in injustice. The size of a monster trial convicts people. The accusations, so much evidence. Jurors couldn't handle it. His first move would be to try to get a new federal trial judge, the eminent Donald Wolfe, to sever the case.

Maybe he should not take the case?

He took it.

Chapter 45

September 13, 2005, Tuesday
Special Session, U.S. District Court
Memphis, Tennessee
To win for their client

One week later, after having lost his motion for severance and all his pretrial motions except one which the court had taken under advisement, Alexander was feeling deeply depressed and disillusioned.

The coal fraud trial was set to begin next week. Yesterday, the judge's secretary had phoned and said all the lawyers should appear in Memphis before the district judge today.

As they filed into the courtroom, the lawyers were buzzing with questions to each other as to the nature of this special session. They were soon to find out. His Honor Judge Wolfe announced he would dismiss all the serious RICO charges and try only the mail fraud charges, whereupon the defense lawyers were delirious with excitement. The Government had been dealt a death blow!

Alexander knew this victory was historical, a first in the United States, and he wrote a letter to one of his friends in Los Angeles, sending him a copy of the ruling and asking that it be included in *The Champion*, the journal of the National Association of Criminal Defense Lawyers.

He had long since lost interest in this organization, because of his view of its *nuts and bolts* approach to the practice of criminal law and its refusal to be concerned about what the law ought to be. But he knew there were some members of this organization who would find this ruling of interest, since it also concerned money and how to make money.

And that was what interested most lawyers! Not changing society or the law. Not looking for new loopholes in the system. The loopholes they were interested in were those designed to win for their client, to make money or earn a fee for themselves, and this was exactly what Alexander was up to in this coal fraud case. Besides, he actually believed his client was innocent. Did lawyers and doctors practice their professions just for money?

Chapter 46

September 19-23, 2005, Monday through Friday
U.S. District Court
Memphis, Tennessee
The definition of justice

The trial began. Some of the defendants pleaded guilty and received sentences from five to twenty years. The seven remaining were going to take their chances with the jury. The Government's proof could still be devastating.

It was agreed at the first evening meeting during the trial that if they could all assert the same defense, it would be the best defense. All but one of the seven lawyers agreed. He chose to alienate himself from the others and to withdraw from the group by putting his chair and that of his client at a separate table, as well as by the manner in which he conducted himself in cross examining—even in making his opening statement.

Alexander knew they had to make the defense simple. He rose to address the jury at the beginning of the trial, and in his opening statement he began by saying, "The coal the Government claims doesn't exist or didn't exist *existed* and still exists today." He added that the coal was in the coal mines in East Tennessee, in the ground his client sold—or, it had been sold and disposed of—although he admitted there were *victims*, that is, there were many people or customers who lost money in the investment. But this was not his client's fault, and the proof would show his client was innocent and the coal was real—that you could still walk up to it and touch coal in those mines.

The other defense lawyers were overjoyed and thankful for Alexander's surprise opening statement, but they kept their composure as they followed suit, like ducks going to a pond, fitting their statements into his opening statement without really saying anything. And off they went.

The prosecution was conducted by a woman, Betty Kelly, who aspired to be the next federal judge in the Western District of Tennessee, but she was totally disorganized from the beginning. Of course, the defense lawyers claimed it was their united, successful front during opening statements and the early stages of the trial which created the disorganization.

They continued to punch the prosecution like prizefighters. Throughout the trial, they cross-examined Government witnesses, "punching" witnesses and knocking the prosecutor off her feet. It soon became evident the defense had control of the case and was winning. The Government was demoralized.

During the trial, the prosecution time and time again tripped, the defendants objecting and the objections being sustained. At night, defense counsel would meet from six until midnight in Alexander's Lincoln American Tower office to map plans and strategies. It was decided to attack every witness and gamble.

Gamble they did, successfully. The trial was a success for the defense. On motion for judgment of acquittal, at the close of the Government's proof, the judge ruled in favor of two of the defendants, and five were left to face the jury, including Alexander's client.

Alexander decided not to call his client as a witness. The Government had failed in its proof, and he had in mind what he wanted to say. Defendants Herbert Spencer, Horance Green, and "Fats" Smith testified. They were the salesmen. The defense closed.

The case would go to the jury with a united defense theory that the Government had failed in its case. Sure enough, as Alexander waited to argue, the Government argued the merits of their case. The defense came back with fury. The case had been taken away from the prosecution.

You could read the jurors' faces. They were leaning toward the defense. All they needed was to be pushed over the edge.

The prosecutor had overstated her case and was relying on the emotion of all the money lost by investors, forgetting the issue: *who caused the loss?* Were these defendants guilty of mail fraud? Conspiracy? *Not my client*, Alexander thought to himself as he rose to address the jury in reply.

"Ladies and gentlemen," he began. "The Sequatchie Valley is a beautiful, ruler-straight chasm bisecting the southern half of the Cumberland Plateau. In fact, the part of the plateau west of the Sequatchie Valley is called by the name commonly applied to the whole, the Cumberland Plateau. East of Sequatchie Valley, it is called Walden Ridge in honor of Elijah Walden, one of the famous bear hunters of the Daniel Boone era." He smiled.

"These mountains are mostly shale, interlayered with numerous coal beds. You heard the Government's own expert admit the coal was there. You heard him testify on cross-examination that coal is made up almost entirely of carbonized plant fragments from plants that grew in ancient swamps much like today's Okefenokee Swamp in Georgia.

"Millions of years of quiet accumulation of plant material followed by deep burial, uplift, and erosion form the mountains of today. You heard the proof. Thick vegetation lives and dies, to fall and sink beneath murky water. Another generation of swamp plants grow atop the old and also die. The accumulating weight squeezes the liquid and gaseous matter out of the lower layers, converting them to peat, a spongy material."

He paused and smiled at the jurors again, hoping to convey his personal interest in the subject. When he knew he had everyone's "scholarly" attention, he continued.

"Then the swamp itself is buried under sediment, compressing even further. What emerges is a layer, thinner and thinner, that is richer and richer in carbon, and poorer in water and hydrocarbons—passing from wood to peat to coal. *To coal.* The coal is there, all except for the coal that was mined and sold to the Utah Mining Company. That's not my client's fault." He continued on, covering every aspect of the proof.

As Alexander leaned against the podium and closed his argument, tears began to come to his eyes, naturally. He now addressed the jurors.

"Ladies and gentlemen, someday I'm going to die, and I hope it's in the Ozark Mountains of Arkansas. Those Ozark mountains are just as beautiful as the mountains of the Sequatchie Valley. From blooming dogwoods and redbuds in the spring to the blaze of bright oranges, reds, and yellows in the fall, the Ozark mountains are alive—like the Sequatchie. There is nothing like the glow of burnt orange leaves in the fall. Rushing streams and rivers. Clear cold water. I'll be moving up there soon, retiring.

"You remember the chicken house that Professor Henry Blank from the University of Tennessee said was out there at Dark Moon mine? Remember, he finally identified it, and it was there. He saw it.

"Well, the coal in those mines up there is just as *real* as that chicken house. It's there. You can touch that coal. Just like you can walk up and touch that chicken house—except the coal at Prince Fred Mine Number Two was stolen and the coal was later mined and sold to the Utah Mining Company. And that coal was also as real as the chicken house!

"When I retire and move to my Ozark farm, and I go out to my little chicken house and pull those eggs out from under those chickens, you know what I hope? I hope I remember—"

Now, tears were streaming down his face, and he wiped his eyes gently with two fingers, then gazed at the jury. "I hope I remember you found my client, David Hill, 'not guilty.' The coal is in the ground. It is as real as my chicken eggs will be on my morning breakfast plate."

The jury was back in 59 minutes. The Government had spent eight million dollars, and much to their shock and chagrin, verdicts of "not guilty" were returned quickly as to each defendant. The judge complimented the defense lawyers, scolded the Government, and adjourned court.

As the defense lawyers stood around congratulating each other and their clients, a Memphis *Commercial Appeal* newspaper reporter, Monk Chastain, filed by and blurted out to Alexander and the other lawyers, "How does it feel to represent guilty defendants who are found *innocent?* Think about all those investors whose money was lost. Millions!"

No one spoke in reply. Alexander knew Chastain understood criminal justice theory, so he felt the question was best left unanswered. Trials were not searches for truth. The system was based upon the philosophical concept that it is far better for 100 guilty men to go free than one innocent man be convicted. Why try to explain that to Chastain?

Of course, the *Commercial Appeal* missed all the important points in the trial. Since the outcome was supposed to be conviction, and this case was designed to get a conviction and to deter others who might engage in conspiracy and mail fraud, it was a disappointment to the Government and the media.

The public would be disturbed. They weren't interested in justice, either. No one really wanted "justice" except the defendants and their lawyers. Lawyers had their own definition of justice: money and legal fees.

Alexander shook his client's hand, and they looked at each other in relief. It had been close.

"I plan now to drill for diamonds at the Crater of Diamonds State Park near Murfreesboro over in Arkansas," Alexander's client began. "I'm interested in a commercial mining venture in Arizona—or Kentucky oil wells. Mr. Alexander, you know anything about legal problems with diamond mines? Oil? Gold?"

As Alexander walked from the courthouse to his office, he thought of how the theory of deterrence actually works. It wasn't a valid reason for convicting people. You could convict anybody and punish them. It didn't have to be a guilty person. You know, put somebody in the court square and cut his hand off—and make everybody watch. Or pour hot liquid on a nude body and make little school children watch on a closed-circuit television.

Or, in the case of murder, strap someone into a large oak chair equipped to spurt thousands of volts of electricity into his body in a current that will run throughout his head from his right leg. Cover his face with a brown leather mask with a triangular opening large enough to expose the nose but covering the eyes, mouth, and chin. Run straps from the forehead section of the mask up over the top of the skull in a vertical arc and horizontally across the eye area. Run another strap across the neck, leaving a bulge of flesh above and below the strap. Raise the right trouser leg to the knee to accommodate the electrical connection.

Turn on the electricity and let others listen to it click—watch his body jolt and stiffen under the straps clamping his arms, chest, and legs to the chair. Watch his clenched fists. Watch his knuckles whiten. Watch his chin and throat turn purple. In a few minutes, see a clear fluid dribble out from under the mask. In five minutes it's all over, the coroner pronouncing death.

Perhaps this would deter other people who watched or heard about the pain and suffering. Force little children to watch. Deter them away from a life of crime.

Then there was the theory of "special" deterrence as opposed to general deterrence, when punishment supposedly deters the guilty individual himself by punishing him.

He couldn't untangle these theories. No theories in criminal justice had actually been proven or established by empirical science or research.

He kept thinking that the real fault in the system was the very foundation of the system—its most basic plank: religion and the doctrine of free will. Criminal justice didn't work. After all, his client might have been guilty, just as the newspaper reporter claimed, and there were certainly innocent people who had been convicted over the years and imprisoned or executed.

The system just didn't work. Even if citizens were rewarded for being good and punished for being bad, it didn't work. Look at the statistics. There had been no decrease in crime in the last hundred years!

Chapter 47

September 26, 2005, Monday
Shelby County Jail
Memphis, Tennessee
Edward Davis

Alexander was on his way to the Shelby County Jail, having received a call from a potential client. His thoughts were on the man he was about to meet. If he took this case, it would be his last, he promised himself. He would try the amygdala case and finally retire.

The trial judge, Walter Hogan, who had been seriously injured in an automobile accident, was out of the hospital and recovering at home. Although he had promised that if he did not "return to the bench soon" he would release his cases for trial by other judges, he had not yet done so. Alexander had decided not to challenge this decision, hoping that the judge's injuries would result in his being more compassionate with defendants such as Armstrong.

In the jail, he began to question Edward Davis about the death of his wife.

"Mr. Davis, did you kill her?"

Alexander had again broken his rule of not asking clients to incriminate themselves.

"No," Davis replied. "I mean, I was there, and I threw gasoline on her right before she burst into flames, but it wasn't my fault."

"Well, I see from the Memphis newspaper that you were accused of throwing the gasoline on her and *then* lighting her with a match."

"That's not what happened, Mr. Alexander. I did throw the gasoline on her. She was harassing me. I was standing at the door of our apartment. We live down in the welfare project. I was washing grease off the door with gasoline and had a small can of gasoline in one hand and a rag in the other. She just kept nagging and nagging. All of a sudden, I just couldn't control myself. I turned around, and I threw the gasoline on her. She had our baby in her arms. I didn't know that, or rather didn't *think*, period. She dropped the baby instantly—I think some of the gas even hit the baby—and she backed up. Just burst into flames. None of the fire got on me or the baby. Wasn't that weird?"

The fee arrangement was made, and Alexander's next stop was the Memphis Police Department, Violent Crimes Section. He would take this case, but no more.

Police Sergeant Bill Haney, an old friend, greeted him. "Alexander, haven't you retired yet? Aren't you tired of being a criminal defense lawyer?"

They looked at each other. Both had bald heads and a bit of gray hair.

Alexander got right to the point. "Haney, what have you got on this Edward Davis? You know, the gasoline death case where the wife burned to death."

"Oh," he said. "You know, I interviewed that woman in the hospital with two officers from the arson squad right before she died. She said he threw a match on her. You know, we airlifted her to Brooke Army Medical Center in San Antonio, Texas, to the Burn Center. She didn't make it. I'm telling you, Alexander, she told me eye-to-eye, face-to-face, that he threw a match on her after he threw the gas."

Alexander left the Violent Crimes office puzzled. He had believed Davis. He wasn't so sure now. Haney would not lie to him. Like his father, who was a police major, Haney was an unusual man with a sterling reputation as a police officer.

Chapter 48

October 3, 2005, Monday
Criminal Court, Shelby County
Memphis, Tennessee
Let your lawyer do the lying

A week later, at the trial of Edward Davis, Alexander was confronted with the police arson photographer who had first appeared on the scene with the firefighters and photographed the scene, returning later at 11:00 p.m., some five hours later, to photograph the scene again. The photographs were eight-by-ten, glossy, black and white, and entered as exhibits.

While the prosecutor put on his proof, Alexander sat looking at the photos. He had already spent hours looking for a clue in those photos. Finally, he heard, "No further questions, Your Honor."

And then, "Your witness, Mr. Alexander."

Rising, he said, "Captain?"

"Yes, sir?"

Alexander had a good relationship with the members of the arson squad. In fact, he had represented one of the captains on a DWI charge which he had won, successfully getting the charges dismissed, and of course earning the respect of the entire arson squad in the process.

He had also impressed them on other occasions with his defense of Jimmy Shotwell, a motorcycle police officer who had been accused of arson. The State in Shotwell's case had introduced five witnesses over a ten-day trial.

The jury had returned a verdict of not guilty. Alexander never understood how, since the victim was *white* and his client was *black*, but they had. He supposed it was because the torch man, who had been convicted earlier as a juvenile delinquent, had escaped from prison and was killed by other teenagers—and therefore was not able to testify against his client. It was a matter of not enough evidence.

His thoughts returned to the Davis trial, and he began again to examine the photographs very closely. He stacked them again in two different piles. One pile contained photographs of a piece of furniture with a match lying on top, clearly visible. The other pile contained the same piece of furniture with no match. He began his cross-examination, not knowing the significance of the match but thinking there would be an obvious explanation by the photographer. For example, maybe they had moved the match and marked it for an exhibit.

"Captain Rodrigues," he began again, "in this set of photographs, there's a match in some and not in others. Could you explain that to the jury, please?" A lawyer should never ask a question to which he doesn't know the answer. He asked anyway.

"Well, yes. The set with the match, those were taken at 11:00 p.m., and those without the match were taken earlier, at 7:00 p.m., at the time the firefighters were putting out the fire."

"Sir, would you repeat that?"

"Yes," the man said, and he repeated his answer.

Alexander had become quite skillful as a trial lawyer, and like Bear Bryant in the fourth inning of a football game, he knew when the punt was blocked and its significance, and he knew what an intercepted pass meant in the closing minutes of a game. He felt the momentum of the trial shift. He now had his theory, and he drove it home with the presentation of his defense. By accident, he had discovered the missing piece of the defense evidence.

Each piece of living room furniture, burnt, charred, and discolored, was placed by Alexander in the courtroom, even the carpet that had been removed. Fortunately, he had caused all these items to be removed and saved, although at the time he did not know why he was doing it.

On the day of the fire, immediately after speaking with Davis at the jail, Alexander had asked Captain Rodrigues to remove and store the items in a mini storage. He brought Rodrigues to testify as to each item. The man was an ex-policeman. He was a good talker, and juries always responded well to him. He was an old man with a lot of integrity.

"Captain Rodrigues, are these items you see in front of you from the fire at the housing project?"

"Yes, sir."

"And did you remove them on my instructions and carefully preserve them in a mini storage located at 403 Union Avenue?"

"Yes, sir, I did. I placed them there and locked the door. I'm the only one with the key."

"And you can positively identify these items?"

"Yes."

Alexander pointed to one of the pieces. "Now, I notice near this piece of furniture you have a hanging lamp lying there. Was that lamp *hanging* at the time of the event?"

"Yes. I removed it upon receipt of your telephone call telling me to take all these items into custody. The police had not marked or preserved the fire crime scene."

"Well, do you remember if the lantern was hanging over this exact piece of furniture?"

"Yes, sir, it was."

"From the ceiling with this long chain hanging down?"

"Yes, sir."

"That's all."

The trap was set. The prosecutor could smell it. He knew the defense would be that static electricity had started the fire. Alexander had disclosed this to him when he was trying to negotiate a plea bargain. The prosecutor refused and instead brought Dr. James Jastrow, the dean of the School of Engineering, University of Memphis, to sit in the courtroom throughout the entire trial. He held a Ph.D. in electrical engineering. He had grown up in Little Rock, Arkansas, Pulaski County.

Pulaski County was named for a Polish nobleman, Count Casimir Pulaski, who left Europe to come to the aid of American revolutionaries, . He was made a brigadier general and was killed in 1779 at the battle of Savannah. "Little Rock" was named by the explorer, Jean Baptiste Bénard de La Harpe, who named the place *La Petite Roche,* "The Little Rock," in 1722. The place grew to be one of diverse views and citizenry.

Alexander was prepared to cross-examine the dean by being friendly and personal. If the dean was called in rebuttal, he would talk about Little Rock, but first he needed his star defense witness.

Alexander called Hans Sparger, a young assistant professor of physics, also from the University of Memphis, who was to be qualified as an expert before the jury. Hans Sparger was a hometown boy, Central High School.

"Doctor Sparger, would you spell your name please?"

"Yes. S-p-a-r-g-e-r."

"Is that Hans Sparger?"

"Yes."

"And you are an assistant professor of physics here at the University of Memphis?"

"That's correct."

"You are from Memphis?"

"Yes. I attended Central High School, played football, and obtained my Ph.D. in physics at the University of Tennessee, Knoxville. My undergraduate degree was from the University of Texas."

"Now, you've testified in court before, haven't you?"

"Yes, a few times."

"And would you just state for the jury your background and credentials, please?"

After his credentials were stated, Alexander moved to qualify the professor as an expert. The motion was granted.

"Dr. Sparger, would you please assume the following facts to be true, then state your opinion to a reasonable degree of scientific certainty as to the cause of the fire?"

Whereupon, Alexander stated the facts as they appeared in the record.

Professor Sparger replied, "My opinion, to a reasonable degree of certainty, is that the cause of the fire was static electricity. You see," he continued, "it's like sliding across the seat of your car, something we've all experienced. That generates a charge of about ten thousand volts and is sufficient to create enough current or spark to cause a fire. When the woman backed into the hanging lamp, the moment before she actually touched the lamp, the spark jumped, and the gas ignited."

Alexander looked around the courtroom and noticed the dean of engineering sitting in the room, listening intently. Alexander hoped the prosecutor would make the mistake of calling this engineer in rebuttal.

"That's all, your Honor, we have no further questions."

The prosecutor's cross-examination of this last defense witness was brief and unsuccessful. Now Alexander waited, like a hungry vulture, for the dean. He would only ask one question on cross-examination: "Doctor Jastrow, assuming the fire was not caused by the *match*, in your opinion, what was the cause of the fire?"

He knew there could be only one possible answer: static electricity. But the prosecutor did not call the dean, and the trial concluded abruptly, followed by very emotional arguments on behalf of both sides. Some of the jurors were crying. Shelby County jurors were, for the most part, good citizens. Alexander hoped they would put aside their bias and not be dishonest.

The jury wasn't out for long, and they came back with a verdict of "not guilty." Alexander was lucky. He had tried the case before honest jurors.

This defendant, Edward Davis, was the maintenance man in the office building across the street from the Lincoln American Tower where Alexander's law office was located. He had also lived in Memphis, a few blocks from Alexander, before he finally retired to Mississippi. He had cut grass and done other jobs in Alexander's Memphis neighborhood.

They would speak, and years later, in fact, he would be introduced to the grandson of this man, the old black man saying, "Son, you always tell your lawyer the truth. Let him do the lying for you," and Alexander had laughed with him. The young boy had grinned, not really knowing what any of it meant.

What Alexander didn't know was that the jury actually prayed to God for direction in rendering their verdict. God had directed "not guilty."

Chapter 49

October 21, 2005, Friday
Criminal Court, Shelby County
Memphis, Tennessee
It was his unconscious brain

It was his first day in court with Major Armstrong's amygdala defense. There had been many delays, other trials, and the trial judge's confinement in the hospital after his automobile accident. His full recovery had been a miracle. But now, finally, the judge was back, and the day had finally arrived. Alexander could assert the amygdala defense.

Alexander was ready. Mike had done a masterful job of preparing Armstrong's pretrial motions, and when the case of William Harrison Armstrong was called, they were ready to do battle. Alexander had decided to give notice of his defense, though he wasn't sure it was required by the Tennessee Rules of Criminal Procedure.

"Your Honor, we are satisfied with the State's discovery. We have the autopsy and all the documents and paper requested. There is nothing in response to our exculpatory motion. We understand. We will rely upon the defense of intoxication and a novel defense, the amygdala defense."

Judge Hogan responded with a roar. "The amygdala defense? Shades of Uncle Remus, Br'er Rabbit, and Tar Baby, too! What's this amygdala defense?"

"Your Honor, it's explained in our trial memorandum."

"I've not had time to read it. You have a hard row to hoe to convince me of such a novel defense. I'm inclined to warn you, I'll probably not accept it. You must be convincing. I'll read your memorandum and rule by written order. Is there anything you want to add, Mr. Alexander?"

Major Armstrong was livid. He had heard "intoxication" and nothing else. He tugged at Mr. Alexander's coat sleeve. "Mr. Alexander, withdraw the intoxication."

"No, Major. I'll explain later."

Willie was mad. Real mad.

Alexander repeated himself on purpose. "Your Honor, we rely upon intoxication as a defense, also."

"I'll allow that," His Honor said in reply.

"But," Alexander continued, "the main defense is the amygdala defense. We admit the killing by the knife in William Harrison Armstrong's hand, but we deny that his conscious brain made that decision. It was his unconscious brain that made that decision to kill. The amygdala did it."

"Do you cite any cases, Mr. Alexander?"

"No, sir. None in our memorandum of law and fact. It is theory. Sound, scientific theory that will be supported by a neurobiologist, a neuroanatomist, and other neuroscientists if allowed at trial. We are serious. We are very serious. Every defense always has its first day in court. The affidavit of our neurobiologist is attached to our memorandum."

Judge Hogan smiled. He liked this lawyer, but he didn't understand this "amygdala" defense.

"I'll rule within twenty days. Clerk, set the case for trial. Everyone understand?"

The prosecutor, Joel Easter, said nothing. He was the best prosecutor on the attorney general's staff. He didn't want to settle this case. He wanted to try it and mash it into Alexander's face. Amygdala defense? *What trash,* he thought. He had tried hundreds of murder cases. No case had ever mentioned any such defense. He had not even heard or read about it.

His Honor then said, "Clerk?"

"November 10, Your Honor," she replied, crossing her legs and turning to avoid Joel Easter's stare.

That lawyer has a dirty mind, she thought.

The jury trial date was the day of the U.S. Marine Corps Birthday. Alexander would miss the annual Birthday Ball. His fellow Marines would hopefully understand.

"Gentlemen, be ready. *Voir dire* will start at 10:00 a.m. promptly. Do not be late. Do not have excuses. This case will be tried. I know the delay has been due to my vehicle accident. I'm not blaming you. No guilty plea or change of plea will be accepted after today."

Joel Easter planned to embarrass Alexander if the judge would allow it.

Alexander left the courtroom and entered the holding area for prisoners just outside the courtroom. Armstrong had told him that he needed to talk.

"It cannot wait," he'd said.

In privacy, Armstrong and Alexander began to argue. A guard stood outside the door.

"I've told you not to use the intoxication defense. I also don't like the amygdala defense. I want you to use, 'I didn't do it. The Mexican did it.'"

Alexander was shocked. "Mexican did what?"

Armstrong explained about the Mexican in the kitchen. He was the cook and dishwasher. "He came out and stabbed Bruce after an argument over loud music. We'd been playing Elvis Presley songs on the juke box for Bruce—over and over. Loud. We were drunk. He stabbed Bruce and fled. I chased him. The bartender did not see what happened. She was in the restroom. She's lying."

"My God, Major, I can't believe it! That's pure fabrication, deception, perjury, lying under oath! I could be disbarred. The jury would laugh at us." Alexander was furious. "Why did you run to Florida?"

"Look, Mr. Alexander, it's my life. I'll decide."

"No, you don't. This is fraud. I'll not do it."

"Really? You've never fabricated a defense?"

Now Alexander was livid. Standing up, face to face with Armstrong, he shouted, "Yes, I have. It worked! In your case, it will *not* work. It's my decision, not yours!"

"Oh, yes! I can fire you."

"Yes, you can."

They both stopped talking. They did not look at one another for a long moment.

Finally, Alexander took a breath and looked directly at Armstrong. He asked, "Am I fired? Yes or no. But before you answer, at least look again at our affidavits from experts. I'll have them soon. And, yes, I'll fabricate for you if you want. Or, you can fire me and get another lawyer. I'll give you the names of those who will *cheat* for you. Be sure you tell them immediately about the Mexican."

They both cooled off. A few minutes later, they were friends again, and Alexander took a kinder tone.

"Let's assume for a moment that we are going to use the amygdala defense. Hear me out. Listen carefully. Why would you explode at the word 'nigger,' be so impulsive to kill?" He waited for an answer.

Armstrong replied, "I don't know, I've been called 'nigger' before—"

Alexander interrupted Armstrong, saying, "Under difference circumstances."

They both just looked at each other.

"What caused you to react so violently against a man you loved? Sergeant Major Bruce Voltz?"

"I don't know. I have felt terrible grief and paid with pain every day since then."

"Were you depressed? You said you were drunk. Had you taken any drugs or medication? Look, let's start at the beginning. I want your entire history again. I'll record it for our experts."

Alexander turned on a tape recorder and placed it on the table. "Ready? Trust me. Begin."

They sat facing each other. Armstrong began. Alexander took little interest until Armstrong started to talk about his father and his father's death.

"He was burned to death in Dyersburg, Tennessee, for a crime he didn't commit! I was there. I remember the courthouse. He was tied to a railroad tie standing up in the courthouse yard. There were several hundred white people. My dad's brother and I were at the back of the crowd. I was just a little boy, but I remember. It was horrible. They were shouting, *'Die, nigger! Die, nigger!'* Some had on KKK white hoods and cloaks, white sheets draped over their horses. It was scary. One of the disguised Klansmen on a horse told us to go, calling us niggers, too."

Alexander remembered the day he'd found the article in the *Dyersburg State Gazette* He had the photo and the editor's affidavit with him. He placed the photo on the table.

"Was this your mother's husband, your actual father? Why didn't you tell me sooner? Why didn't your grandmother tell me?"

"She told me to never mention I was his son—the son of someone accused of being a child rapist. A 13-year-old white girl. He wasn't guilty, according to my uncle. We always pretended the whole thing never happened. I forgot about it until today."

"Did you believe, as a child, that your dad was innocent?"

"I did."

Alexander wondered if he was being truthful.

This might be the trigger I'm looking for, Alexander thought. *This kind of memory is colored by the amygdala.*

"Now, tell me the rest of your life story."

Armstrong started talking, but Alexander was no longer listening. He was sure he had what he needed.

Three professionals, Dr. DuBois, Dr. Wilkens, and Dr. Vann Smith, a neuropsychologist, had each agreed to testify, and Alexander had made each an "ethical" fee arrangement. The fee could not be excessive or contingent. Besides, if "excessive," jurors would question opinions based upon a large sum of money, thinking the opinions were bought and paid for.

The tape of Armstrong telling his story would be duplicated and sent to the doctors tomorrow by UPS overnight. A letter of explanation would be included.

It had been a good day for Alexander. Hopefully, his client would forget "the Mexican did it" defense. Armstrong had restated his life history, and it was as told before to Alexander—except for the addition of the eyewitness account of the burning of his father by the KKK. He decided that Armstrong was indeed telling the truth.

But why had Armstrong not originally disclosed his father's execution, the facts surrounding this horrible childhood experience? Was there something else behind that omission? *He did say he'd forgotten about it until now. To witness such horror as a little boy and then to have to pretend it never happened? Unimaginable....*

Back in his office, Alexander told himself that he would be prepared. His Honor had not yet ruled against him. Would His Honor's order recognize his theories? Or, would it warn him not to argue the amygdala defense? Perhaps he would allow the amygdala defense. Alexander thought to himself that the problem was that his only other defense was intoxication, and Willie Armstrong didn't want it used and was still boiling mad about it!

Chapter 50

November 2, 2005, Wednesday
Shelby County Jail
Memphis, Tennessee
The unbiased juror does not exist

Alexander had set aside a day to meet Willie in the jail to further discuss this issue. That day had arrived. He had taken the elevator from his office to Main Street and walked down Main, turning on Washington to the jail. It took 15 minutes. It seemed like an eternity.

Inside the jail at the Criminal Justice Center, he waited for Willie in the attorney-client visiting room. He knew there was going to be a heated argument. Willie arrived, unsmiling, attired in an orange prison jumpsuit. He sat down.

Alexander began. "You don't understand—"

"Yes, I understand. You will not humiliate me, or my father, or my family. I may be an alcoholic, but I'm a decorated Marine." He was. This was the first time he had said this to Alexander in such a manner. It seemed strange. "And no, you'll not degrade us."

"Willie, if you don't let me argue intoxication, it might mean the rest of your life will be spent in prison."

They both remained silent for just a moment.

Willie didn't back down. "No, no. I'll go to prison for life first. Do you understand what I'm saying?"

"No, I don't," Alexander replied. "Explain it."

"It's my life. It's my trial."

"Willie, as your lawyer, I've got to decide the theory of the defense and the tactics, not you."

"Over my dead body. You say one word about intoxication, and I'll silence you with one blow. I don't need a knife." That last statement was almost a growl.

Alexander was seeing another Willie Armstrong. This was another person! Did he have two—or more than two—personalities?

Alexander was now scared. This was one hell of a man. He had no desire to fight him. He remembered the amygdala. He remembered the effect of low serotonin.

"Okay, Major, you win. No intoxication."

Alexander lied. He would use the defense anyway if he had to, by surprise.

"See you in court, Willie. Last visit. Be sure you put on your new striped blue suit and red USMC tie. Best shoes, haircut, bath, and a smile."

Willie left. He refused to shake Alexander's outstretched hand. He didn't smile.

He was still angry.

As Armstrong left the jail on his way to his office, he began to plan *voir dire*. The bias of the jury was the problem. Regardless of the defense, race was an issue. How could he excuse the racists? He would find a way to level the playing field.

To hell with the Constitution at this point. To hell with Batson v. Kentucky except as it applied to the prosecutor. If he caught the prosecution cheating, he would scream to high heaven. But he would cheat, regardless. It was not unethical—just unconstitutional, according to the Batson decision—for him to excuse jurors based on race alone. Was it? He didn't care.

It was time to organize focus groups. He now had his theories of the defense. Bias or dishonesty of jurors could be partially exposed by pretrial focus groups. Pretrial focus groups find: (1) which demographics will most likely produce the ideal juror; (2) which demographics will produce the worst juror; (3) what themes should be utilized at trial; (4) what arguments have the most appeal against the defendant;

(5) what arguments have the most appeal for the defendant; (6) what is the weakness of the case; and (7) the issue of racial bias.

Which type of focus group should he use? Adversarial, neutral, or concept? An adversarial focus group receives a presentation for each side of the case, discusses the case with the moderator, and then deliberates. In a neutral focus group, the participants hear a presentation by the moderator/presenter representing both sides' contentions, discuss with the moderator/presenter, and then deliberate. With a concept, or brainstorming focus group, there is no formal presentation of each side's position; rather, the moderator and the participants have a focused discussion about aspects of the case. He would use all three, in three different groups, at Germantown Methodist Church.

Alexander realized a trial is not a search for the truth. Facts are not presented to the jury by rules of evidence to arrive at truth. Differing human perceptions about an event are presented by the art and science of communications to arrive at *justice*. *Justice* is the decision of the jury.

The unbiased juror does not exist. The concept that jurors are people whose minds and behavioral dispositions will allow them to weigh evidence impartially does not have psychological or practical relevance. Verdicts are based upon (1) bias of jurors before trial; (2) irrelevant and inadmissible information acquired during trial; and (3) relevant and admissible evidence. Citizens, jurors, and judges see criminal responsibility quite differently.

He remembered the words of Sir Edward Marshall Hall, a British lawyer (1858-1927):

> *"My profession and that of an actor are*
> *somewhat akin, except that I have no scenes to*
> *help me, and no words are written for me to say.*

There is no blackcloth to increase the illusion. There is no curtain. But, out of the vivid, living dream of somebody else's life, I have to create an atmosphere—for that is advocacy."

Chapter 51

November 10, 2005, Thursday
Criminal Court, Shelby County
Memphis, Tennessee
A surprise witness

The trial of William Harrison Armstrong had begun. Alexander and the prosecutor, Joel Easter, were at the bench outside the hearing of the jury, so long as they whispered. Alexander was addressing the judge. "Your Honor, the prosecutor has excused nine *black* jurors out of this panel. I object under Batson." The trial had indeed begun.

The prosecutor whispered back. The court reporter was recording the entire event. Court TV was there. The courtroom was packed.

Alexander whispered, "I'm objecting not only because they are *black,* but because this is a bogus death penalty case." The prosecutor was silent.

"Your Honor, this is a sham," Alexander began again. "He has no grounds for the death penalty. He has no statutory aggravating factors. His claims of *torture* are false. There are no facts. There is no such evidence."

Judge Hogan replied, "Mr. Alexander, I'm the judge. I've ruled. Now go back to your seat. Your objections are overruled."

Armstrong was so mad he almost blurted out what an idiot the judge was, but he didn't want a mistrial or to go to jail for contempt.

He returned to his seat and looked at Willie. He could see the worried look on the man's face.

"Don't worry, Willie. We're okay."

Willie looked like the President of the United States. Or a picture poster of a U.S. Marine colonel. No military uniform. His suit and tie were perfect. Dark, charcoal gray, and a USMC tie—something about "God, honor, and country" in the tie. What happened to the dark blue suit he was supposed to wear?

Alexander was proud of his client. But what would happen at his first mention of intoxication? *Oh, my. ...*

It had taken three days to get the jury. He could not mention his amygdala defense or argue it. He could not mention (yet) his intoxication defense. Instead, he had hammered away that a juror had *two* duties—not just to convict the guilty, but to also protect the innocent. If the proof showed "not guilty," would they protect Major Armstrong?

Alexander had a surprise witness—Sergeant Rodney "Rocky" Baugh, a Marine from Major Armstrong's earliest days, before Armstrong had become an officer. Baugh had been stationed with Armstrong, John McKenzie, and Bruce Voltz in Sicily at the nuclear weapons facility.

Baugh had known Bruce Voltz well, and he said Bruce was a racist. Bruce hid it, rarely admitting or showing his prejudice. Ironically, Bruce was Rodney's good friend and also Major Armstrong's—a black man. Bruce had confided in "Rocky" that he was trying to rid himself of being a racist.

How would Alexander use this witness? These new facts? Could he cheat?

Alexander recalled his interview with Baugh.

Baugh's grandparents on both sides of his family were German and lived in Ohio and Pennsylvania. Rodney believed Armstrong was the best Marine he had ever met. "A man of unbelievable courage," he'd said. Rodney related war games they had played together.

Baugh, Armstrong, Voltz, and McKenzie had all been transferred to the 4th Marines. Armstrong was accepted for Officer's Candidate School, Quantico, Virginia, and came back as platoon leader, Charlie Company, First Battalion, 4th

Marines. All four became good buddies, except Armstrong was now *Lieutenant* Armstrong.

Rodney had a photo of Armstrong, Bruce Voltz, and himself from the time they were stationed in Sicily.

"He risked his life for ours. I wasn't with him in Central America when he got the Silver Star. I had left the Corps and gone back to college. I graduated from the University of Florida. I have my own computer sales company in Tampa. I can come to trial on a moment's notice.

"Will I get to see Armstrong today? I heard he fled to Florida—Orlando—after he killed Bruce. I think he was looking for me, but I had moved from Orlando to Tampa. I came out a Sergeant E-5.

"Bruce Voltz stayed in. He came out and retired as a sergeant major. I heard he was in the Central America ambushes with Major Armstrong. It was a secret mission. To this day, I don't know the details. All I know is Armstrong got the Silver Star. His grandmother mailed me a copy of the news photo."

Alexander was astonished. What a witness. Married, two children, picture perfect witness. He was a self-made millionaire. Rodney Baugh would blow the prosecution away. He was the best character witness Alexander had ever met, not only as to his opinions, but he knew Armstrong's character. He could not be successfully cross-examined, and Alexander could "teach" him how to "explode" facts on cross-exam. He'd be good at it. This was dynamite.

Alexander knew that all of his character witnesses would need to be taught the questions and answers to questions in order for the character testimony to be admissible.

"Truthfulness" was the issue. He would work with each independent of the others, then in a group. He would use all of them (if he could) and instruct them on how to "back-fire" when cross-examined.

He still had much to do.

Chapter 52

November 15, 2005, Tuesday
Criminal Court, Shelby County
Memphis, Tennessee
The rules of discovery

The trial continued. The Iraq war occupied everyone's concerns and attention. It was no ordinary distraction. Now, Alexander could use it. His client was a war hero. A courageous man. But Alexander knew he was in trouble.

His Honor had denied his amygdala defense as not supported by law, and he had ruled against the use of one of Alexander's character witnesses for lack of timely notice, a discovery error. Rodney Baugh, his best character witness, could not testify! This would be an issue on appeal if Armstrong was convicted.

At a second trial, he would call Rodney. He had also preserved the issue of the prosecutor's illegal excuse of black jurors. He was sure this would reverse any convictions. He would also pressure the denial of the amygdala defense as an appeal issue if Armstrong was convicted.

Alexander was angry about the discovery error. He knew the rules of discovery were for the purpose of fairness, and certainly it was fair to require both sides to not operate "trial by ambush" and surprise. This was now an appeal issue. He had tried to cheat, and it had failed.

Alexander could also assert the intoxication defense and attempt to "knock out" first-degree murder as provided by Tennessee law, but Armstrong would still face lesser included offenses of second-degree murder and voluntary and involuntary manslaughter. Alexander would have no choice.

Alexander tore to shreds the order denying the use of the amygdala defense. He was crushed. He had already decided to call a psychiatrist on the intoxication issue and had researched Armstrong's family tree, looking for alcoholics. He was certain it was genetic in origin. The barmaid would establish the amount of alcohol. He could do it without Armstrong's testimony.

If Armstrong got belligerent, he could be removed from the courtroom by the judge. He hoped, of course, that if this occurred, it would occur outside the presence of the jury.

Chapter 53

November 16, 2005, Wednesday
Criminal Court, Shelby County
Memphis, Tennessee
A dispute between lawyer and client

Armstrong exploded. "I told you, Alexander, we are not going there—no intoxication defense!"

"It isn't really a defense," replied Alexander. "This evidence will reduce the killing to no more than second-degree murder. Listen. No more outbursts or interruptions."

"I can't do that," said Armstrong.

Alexander talked to the judge. His Honor, looking at Armstrong, said, "Mr. Bailiff, take him from the courtroom. We shall proceed."

"No, you listen!" interrupted Armstrong.

He was rushed out of the courtroom by the deputies.

Alexander turned around and sat down at the table.

After the judge had excused the jury, he called Major Armstrong back into the courtroom.

"Your Honor, we have a problem," explained Alexander. "A dispute between lawyer and client. Can you resolve it?"

"Yes," replied the judge. "Mr. Armstrong, you will again be excused from the courtroom if you do not follow my instructions. You will be allowed to return if you sincerely promise not to explode or excite the jury. Do you understand?"

Armstrong said nothing. He looked at the judge with contempt. Judge Hogan ordered Armstrong removed. Alexander proceeded with the intoxication defense and called his first witness.

Alexander knew he had a good appeal issue in the denial of the amygdala defense and also in the selection of the jury.

Batson had been violated. The prosecutor had wrongfully excluded nine black jurors!

Now the judge had banned Armstrong from the courtroom. Would this be a good issue? How? Would it be a reversible error?

Chapter 54

November 17, 2005, Thursday
Criminal Court, Shelby County
Memphis, Tennessee
A verdict

The trial was finally over. The prosecution had mostly gotten its way, and Alexander had called only one expert witness to explain intoxication and the genetic link of alcoholism. His Honor had allowed the expert opinion testimony over the objection of the prosecutor.

Armstrong did not testify and did not return to the courtroom. Motions and final argument had concluded. The jury was "deliberating."

Alexander wanted to talk to Armstrong, but he decided Armstrong might explode and kill him. Alexander was afraid to go into the holding cell with him.

After almost three hours of deliberation, the jury signaled they had a verdict and returned. The foreman announced Armstrong as guilty of first-degree murder.

After discharging the jury, His Honor allowed Armstrong to return.

"Mr. Armstrong, you have been found guilty of first-degree murder. You are to be returned to the Shelby County Jail. I'll set post-trial motions for a hearing in 30 days. Bail is, of course, denied. Do you have anything you wish to say?"

Armstrong shook his head. "No."

Alexander's mind was racing. Seven women and five men had been "selected" to hear the evidence against Armstrong. Of course, "selection" referred to weeding out unwanted jurors from the group of candidates chosen and sent over by the clerk's office. Besides all nine black jurors having been excused, where did Alexander go wrong? The jury had been sequestered. Was his failure because of bad publicity before the trial?

The judge had identified and excused the alternative jurors at the end of the proof stage of the trial by a random-selection process. The jurors had all been over the age of 30. One panel member was 70. This juror had elected not to claim an automatic age exemption.

He considered the women on the jury—a chemist, an office manager, a telephone company employee, a state employee, a financial analyst, a critical care nurse, and a department store clerk. Male jurors included two Army veterans, a public schoolteacher, a state special education executive, and an elementary school teacher-coach. Where had he gone wrong?

Intoxication? It didn't work. Would the verdict have been different had Armstrong been allowed the amygdala defense? Did he "pick" the wrong jurors? What if the jury had been a mix of white and black? Alexander would appeal. Seek a second trial. Hope.

What would he do if there was a second trial? Or, third? He had used juror questionnaires and a jury consultant. Was this wrong? His focus groups? What went wrong—if anything?

He did not dare try to talk to Major Armstrong. He would start to work on post-trial motions and the appeal immediately.

Chapter 55

December 20, 2005, Tuesday
Brushy Mountain State Prison
Petros, Tennessee
Not just a client

Armstrong had not had any visitors. He was locked up for life with the slim possibility of parole, if his conviction was not set aside on appeal to the Tennessee Court of Criminal Appeal in Jackson. He had appeared for the post-trial motions hearings.

Alexander's motion for a new trial was denied, but all the issues for appeal had been preserved. A motion for judgment of acquittal was also denied, including an application for reduction of sentence to second-degree murder. Alexander believed His Honor might reduce the sentence, but he didn't. It was just another appellate issue now.

Armstrong was still angry at Alexander about the intoxication defense. They hadn't spoken since he was removed from court during the trial. No letters, either, although Alexander had dutifully mailed Armstrong copies of each motion and memorandum, as well as a cover letter of apology for the disagreement. Alexander still claimed it was his decision and not that of his client.

Alexander had hoped the conviction would be reversed or at a minimum reduced to second-degree murder and remanded for a sentencing hearing. He hoped for, say, a forty-year sentence with all the standard conditions of "good time," parole, and so on. With all his possible credits, Armstrong might be able to return to society before he died.

Alexander was depressed. What a way to end a career. He had never cared more for a client. Armstrong had become a friend—not just a client.

Chapter 56

December 22, 2005, Thursday
A three-judge panel
Jackson, Tennessee
The night riders

Alexander made a good argument when he appeared before the three-judge panel in Jackson, Tennessee, to argue the issues on appeal. As he researched the issues for Armstrong's brief, he had recalled reading about the Tennessee "night riders" case. He had first heard of the night riders from his grandmother when he was a teenager.

Reelfoot Lake in Lake and Obion counties, in Northwest Tennessee, was created by the action of a series of earthquakes that centered around New Madrid, Missouri, from 1811 to 1812. The titles to that land remained in effect through sale and inheritance, but the local farmers, fisherman, and landowners cooperatively used it as a common resource for food and income.

In the 1860s, J. C. Burdick leased a portion to run a fishing business on Reelfoot Lake. Later, a group of men came in from Kentucky who bought lake property and attempted to restrict the use of their land to only their club. These actions enraged the locals, who had always considered the lake common property.

Soon after the Civil War, a man named James C. Harris moved to the area and built his fortune on land acquisition—clearing timber, draining swamps, cultivating cotton, and then investing in more land. Though considered a great success in some men's eyes, to the agrarian community he was an enemy eager to kill their way of life for his own profit. They tried protests, legal actions, and physical threats, to no avail.

By 1898, Harris had acquired most of the deeds for the land under Reelfoot Lake, and he planned to drain it, as well. Harris died in 1903, and his son inherited his father's land. He then went to court to try to prevent anyone from using the land without permission. Three lawyers, including Captain Quentin Rankin and Colonel Robert Z. Taylor, argued against this and won. This was an apparent win for the locals. But in 1907, Rankin and Taylor purchased the remaining deeds and forced the creation of the West Tennessee Land Company, an act of betrayal that the locals would never forgive.

In the spring of 1908, the Tennessee Supreme Court ruled that Reelfoot Lake was subject to private ownership. In response to what was seen as an egregiously intolerable takeover of their land and livelihood, a group of men banded together, their actions mirroring those of the "night riders" who were fighting against supporters of the American Tobacco Company in western Kentucky and Tennessee. Though their terrorist actions were illegal and destructive, many citizens supported their cause. Politics and the social, economic, and racial upheaval of the time all played their part.

The "night riders" in the vicinity of Reelfoot Lake rode around taking their vengeance and creating fear in rather unusual and cruel ways. Besides the general attacks on people associated with the West Tennessee Land Company and those who supported them, including the black population who provided cheap labor for the cotton industry, they did such things as lynching an entire black family of five, forcing one of the partners of the fishing dock to carry gasoline to the dock to burn it down, and forcing another man—who refused to do their work—to plow a field like a mule, after which they sent him to a barn to be whipped.

This went on for about seven months. It wasn't until the murder of Quentin Rankin that the governor stepped in. Masked riders had kidnapped Rankin and Taylor, and

Rankin was murdered at the edge of Reelfoot Lake. His body was found hanged and riddled with bullets. He wore a gray suit, white shirt, and a tie. Taylor had escaped through the swamp.

Governor Malcom Patterson ordered an investigation into the murder and sent in the National Guard to keep order. Eventually, six were found guilty in the murder of Quinton Rankin and sentenced to death. In 1909, the appeal was argued before the Supreme Court of Tennessee sitting at Jackson. The defendant prisoners were present, neatly dressed. It was raining outside. The defense lawyer made technical arguments. The Tennessee Supreme Court overturned their convictions.

The opinion found errors in the organization and selection of the grand jury. The court also found error in the ruling of the trial judge to disallow 24 challenges for each defendant and other errors. The trial judge's attempt to "short-cut" the procedure was error. The denial of the challenge to juror White (for cause) was also error.

The murder had grown out of a "lawless spirit," but there were many who were sympathetic as well as those who condemned the reversal of the convictions. Many realized that when men who were once productive citizens are faced with the despair of being deprived of their livelihood by another, they can easily resort to trying to take the law into their own hands. The *Memphis Commercial Appeal* claimed it was a "bad day for justice" and a "triumph for murder and lawlessness."

From a man's ambition to buy Reelfoot Lake and drain part of it to harvest the timber and establish farmland, came the lawlessness of the night riders, murder, and convictions that were reversed by the Tennessee Supreme Court. Eventually, this led to state ownership of Reelfoot Lake in 1914. In the 1960s, it was designated as a U.S. National Natural Landmark by the National Park Service.

Without knowing the history of the area, no one could ever imagine the murderous time that had led to this quiet place, so perfect for nesting bald eagles and cypress trees. Why was he remembering this case? Hopefully, Armstrong's conviction would also be set aside. Alexander had cited the night riders' reversal in his brief. Nine black jurors in Armstrong's case had been excused illegally. The principle of law was the same in both cases.

Fortunately, there were lots of Tennessee and federal cases on point—not just that of the night riders. Surely, Armstrong's case would also be reversed, and he would get another trial.

Chapter 57

July 14, 2006, Friday
Office of John Alexander
Memphis, Tennessee
Shocked beyond belief

It was Friday, a warm summer day—not too hot, somewhere in the high 80s, and there had been a nice breeze this morning that cut back the usual Memphis humidity that came in from the Gulf of Mexico. Six months had passed since Alexander had argued the issues on appeal in Jackson, Tennessee.

He sat at his desk at the Lincoln American Tower. A copy of the *Opinion of the Tennessee Court of Criminal Appeals* had arrived in the U.S. mail. Alexander slowly opened the big envelope.

"Reversed."

He was shocked beyond belief. Good news. He read the *Opinion* quietly, and then told Ann to get the Warden's Office at Brushy Mountain on the telephone. The Court had in fact recognized the novel amygdala defense! Armstrong had been granted a new trial with reasonable bail. Alexander could introduce his proof, his experts could testify, and he could argue the amygdala defense.

The *Opinion* cited the "night riders" case and others cited by Alexander in his brief. The Court had also reversed the conviction because of the illegal excuse of the black jurors. Another great victory. Would Armstrong listen?

What great news. He would retire, but first he would retry this case—if Armstrong would have him.

"Get him on the phone, Ann. Now."

"I've got the Warden's Office on the phone, John," she said in a grim, forceful tone.

He picked up the phone.

"Hello, Warden. This is John Alexander. I need to talk to my client, William Harrison Armstrong. Can you arrange that as soon as possible?"

There was a slight pause. "Mr. Alexander, Mr. Armstrong was found dead in his cell this morning. Cause of death is unknown. It was suicide, we believe…."

Alexander hung up the phone. It was the worst message he had ever received in his life. He would retire now—no question.

Life would never be the same.

Armstrong had left a letter in his cell addressed to Alexander. The warden stamped it and put it in the mail.

#

About the Author

EDWARD WITT CHANDLER is a retired Tennessee criminal defense lawyer who now lives in the Ozark Mountains of Arkansas. In the late 1960s, he was one of the first three full-time public defenders in Shelby County, Tennessee. He was a criminal defense lawyer in the trenches of the war against crime for over 40 years.

Chandler holds a B.S. from Bethel College 1963 and is a graduate of Vanderbilt University 1967 (J.D.) and the University of Washington 1978 (LL.M.). He completed his military obligation in the U.S. Marine Corps. He was also an assistant professor of criminal justice, University of Memphis 1976-1977, and an adjunct member of the faculty for several years. He has been a lecturer at continuing legal education seminars for lawyers in Tennessee, Arkansas, Missouri, and Texas.

On November 13, 1985, Chandler presented a paper entitled "Cloning Criminals: The Death of the Doctrine of Free Will" to the American Society of Criminology's 37th

Annual Meeting in San Diego, California. His articles include "A Crime Free Society: Genetic Engineering: Will It Be a Viable Solution to Curb our Nation's Rising Crime Problem?" (*Memphis Press-Scimitar,* October 3, 1983); "A Criminal-Free Society Through Gene Splicing" (*The Commercial Appeal*, March 31, 1985); "Sex, Death and Lawyer's Ethics" (*ATLA Docket*, June 1998); and "The Genetic Defect Defense" (*ATLA Docket*, Arkansas Trial Lawyers Association, Spring 1999).

Chandler's first non-fiction book, *Understanding Crime: Why we took the wrong road in the war against crime,* was published in 2019. This book was the result of his observations in the trenches of the "War Against Crime" as a criminal defense lawyer, as well as his research covering the causes of crime, which culminated in his conclusion as to where we went wrong in our understanding of "crime" and "punishment"—and what we need to do about it.

Author's Note

While this book is, in large part, a work of fiction, and the characters and businesses are not real, the concepts of the amygdala defense as outlined in the story are very real, relevant, and timely.

Reference is made to actual written pieces, such as quotes by Charles Dickens, the 1982 report commissioned by President Carter and presented to President Reagan (*Splicing Life: A Report on the Social and Ethical Issues of Genetic Engineering with Human Beings*), and an article from *Newsweek*.

Certain events and groups are also mentioned in this book, including the KKK and the night riders of the Reelfoot Lake area in Tennessee. Care was taken to describe historical events in the truest manner possible using current reference materials.

Readers are encouraged to further their own knowledge through research and travel, and to keep their eyes and minds open as they apply critical thought, one of the most valuable assets of human life, to all they encounter.

Edward Witt Chandler, March 2021